Life's Evil Twin

A simple man struggles with death after near
death experiences while being recruited for the
family business.

Christopher J. Stone

Edited by Samantha Ondyak

ISBN-10: 1938634756
ISBN-13: 978-1-938634-75-8

DEDICATION

To my co-worker who has since passed on
and gave me the insight and desire to write
this. To my good friend that passed away as
a child and I still miss every day. To every
teacher that helped me and gave me the
intellectual tools to write this book. To one
particular individual who did a lot for me,
Terry Kemmer at Mayville. And lastly, to my
Dad. We did not always see eye to eye but
you were my Dad, rest in peace.

Christopher Stone

Life's Evil Twin

By Christopher J. Stone

For more books like this one, visit Christopher J. Stone's website at:
http://christopherjstone.com/
2012 copyright by Freedom of Speech Publishing, Inc.

Printed in the United States of America
The publisher offers discounts on this book when ordered in bulk quantities. For more information, contact Sales Department, Phone 815-290-9605, Email:
sales@fospub.com

Product and company names mentioned herein are the trademarks or registered trademarks of their respective owners.

Freedom of Speech Publishing, Leawood KS, 66224
www.fospub.com

ISBN-10: 1938634756
ISBN-13: 978-1-938634-75-8

A SPECIAL THANK YOU TO YOU!

On behalf of everyone at Freedom Of Speech Publishing, thank you for choosing Life's Evil Twin for your reading enjoyment.

As an added bonus and special thank you, for purchasing Life's Evil Twin, you can enjoy discounts and special promotions on other Freedom of Speech Publishing products. Visit www.fospub.com/vip to learn more.

We are committed to providing you with the highest level of customer satisfaction possible. If for any reason you have questions or comments, we are delighted to hear from you. Email us at cs@fospub.com or visit our website at: http://fospub.com/contact-us-2/.

If you enjoyed Life's Evil Twin, visit www.fospub.com for a list of similar books
or upcoming books.

Again, thank you for your patronage. We look forward to providing you more entertainment in the future.

Contents

Chapter One
Fall is Here

The brisk autumn air blew lightly through the weathered maple trees, making the leaves dance and play in the bright sunlight. Occasionally, a leaf would begin to spin so quickly that it snapped from its branch and lolled listlessly to the ground in slow circles, caught on the breeze. The fallen leaves would scuttle along the park's walkway, as if running from the footsteps of the old man strolling down the shaded path. The large trees rocketed to the sky throughout the park and spilled into the city around it. The old man realized that the bowers were probably the only thing in the park older than he was. They had been there when his own father had brought him there to play as a young boy. They had been there when he sought a retreat from the busy world on a bench beneath them for a sandwich and soda. They had been there when he brought his late wife on their first date for some quiet time away from the world. They had been there when he brought his own son to romp on the playground in a clearing amidst the copses. And they were there now, on his daily stroll.

The park was located in the heart of a sleepy Midwestern town. The old man had grown to love and hate the place—funny how you can do that at the same time. It reminded him of his younger days: like a drunk who hated what the beer did to him, but could not stop himself from drinking each night. The park called to him, and he responded. The memories were bittersweet in his old age, but they were his story. He walked through the park each day to relive them, despite the twinge of regret and loss that came along with them. He hated it and loved it. Somehow he felt stuck here, like the man in *Hotel California*. But then again, he also felt safe. He had given up the excitement of big city life for a life of safety. Isn't that why people live in small towns, anyway? To find a place where they can avoid crime and safely walk in the park?

What a great day, he thought to himself. He could have said it out loud, but no one would have heard. He hugged his light jacket closer to himself—not because it was cold, but because the wind picked up at times and whipped against the back of his neck. Despite the breeze, the sun beamed down brilliantly. It was one of those days you enjoy because the heat of the summer has been broken but the bitter cold of winter has not set in yet. It was one of those days when your body seems to let off the heat it has been storing from the hot summer days, as if your body was a big rock that sat in the hot summer sun all day, and now was releasing the heat that had been built up. It was one of those days that just felt good.

The old man was busy with his thoughts. He had time for those thoughts, now, but few others to share them with, so he took the time to share them with himself. Sad in a way—he had so much to teach at his age, so much knowledge built up through the years to pass on, but no-one to teach it to. Instead, he decided to re-teach himself before his time ran out or his mind became un-teachable—before age took its toll. The old man had considered volunteering with a charitable organization, but he had no time for that—time for everything else, but not that.

The younger generation had no time for him, so why should he have time for them? As he sat in the park each day, they could have said hello as they rushed by. He would have been glad to tell them anything they might need to know, if they just asked. But most of them believed they had nothing to learn from the past. The new way of doing business was the key. They would pay big money for motivational speakers, and focus groups, and independent contractors to come into their businesses to merely reinforce their belief that success lay in progress, not in the past. The old man had long ago learned that, if you pay the right amount of money, he will tell you what you want to hear or agree with you. He could tell them what they need to know about life if they wanted it; he could tell them that everything "new" is just something old repackaged in a new wrapper. But they didn't want to hear that. So the old man kept his thoughts to himself.

As he continued down the path, the old man noticed a few toys lying haphazardly around the once-busy playground: a hula-hoop entangled in a shrub, a broken shovel next to the sandbox, an empty juice box sitting on a picnic table, a slowly deflating soccer ball under the see-saw. *For a nice day, the park should be full of playful kids*, the old man mused; *parks need kids in them, as they need the trees and grass.* But the kids were back in school for the year, and the forgotten toys provided the only sign that the children had once been there.

Aside from the old man, the only people in the park seemed to be using it as a shortcut on their hurried paths from one office building to another office building on the other side of the commons, hurrying from one appointment to another. The old man wondered if they wouldn't rather spend more time outside on such a beautiful day. Perhaps they'd rather not think about the blissful atmosphere. They had to keep busy, not stop or notice an old man enjoying the day. If they did, they might not be able to make themselves go into the buildings to keep their appointments. The old man knew that, someday, those important appointments would not matter, those appointments that, today, seemed to be so imperative that the world would end if they did not make them. He thought back to all of the appointments he had made throughout his life. How many of them really mattered? How many shifted the world in significant ways? How many made him in to the old man he was now? Not many. He wanted to tell the young men to slow down, to enjoy the light breeze and the glorious sun, to listen to the sparrows singing in the branches as the maple leaves turned brilliant shades of crimson and orange and fell to the ground. But he didn't tell them any of those things. And they wouldn't have listened to him if he had.

He walked slowly through the park, taking his time to watch everything, soaking up the day and drinking everything in. He was long retired from the rat race and, at his age, he had learned to enjoy every moment of the day as if it was some kind of comfort food. Each bit was to be enjoyed, savoring the taste in his mouth for as long as he could and letting it flood his mind with memories of better times. There were a number of things he had enjoyed throughout his life that he could no longer experience since his doctor had put them on a list of things he should not do or eat. But this, a great day and a slow walk in the park, he could still enjoy, and he was going to do just that.

At one point, the old man had been like those busy businessmen. He had rushed through his life, trying to get to the end. He had played life like a game of Monopoly, frantically trying to buy up as many properties as possible, bankrupt his competitor, and cross the finish line before the others. Now, he realized that the end is never where you think it will be. Sometimes it's a letdown. Most of the time, it's lonely. Whether you come in first or last, all of the pieces have to back into the box at the end of the game. As most old men knew, rushing to finish the game only meant that another game had to begin, and that you had to set up all of the pieces of that new game, learn its rules, and, once again, rush through it in a fruitless attempt to be the winner. Then the cycle starts anew. This particular old man had not checked out of the game. Rather, he had decided to play on his own terms. He would enjoy his stay on Boardwalk, revel in the sights at Marvin Gardens, and grab a drink at the local bar on Mediterranean Avenue. Coming in first didn't matter anymore. He was going to play slowly and leisurely, enjoying the game itself, not anticipating what was to come. So on that cool autumn day, the old man strolled through the park and enjoyed all of the bits the other players didn't see.

Walking along the path, he spotted a well-used bench and lowered his body onto the wooden seat. He couldn't tell whether the creaking came from the sagging wood or his back, but he decided not to think about that. Instead, he pulled an old keychain out of his jacket's left pocket and looked long and deeply at it, rubbing his wrinkled fingers over the dark stone. The silver metal surrounding the stone showed signs of tarnish, but the patina only spoke to the fact that the totem had obviously been well used by its owner, and the owner before him, and the owner before him. The pointed edges had been worn down and smoothed off over time. The coin-sized stone in the middle looked like some kind of dark birthstone that glistened in the sunlight but appeared to be just a regular black stone in the shade.

Even to an untrained jeweler's eye, it was obvious that the keepsake had not always been a keychain. The signs of wear made it clear that the piece was much older than any new technology requiring a key. The old man closed his eyes as he fingered every groove of the relic. He knew exactly how to trace the shape of the hauntingly colored stone, the outline of the metal, and the slight fissures that came from years of use. The keychain needed a good cleaning, but the old man had could never entrust it to another, even if it meant returning the piece to its former glory with a solid polishing. And weren't the discolorations and imperfections part of its charm? Wasn't there a memory attached to every scratch? It would be sinful to buff and wash them all away. It was best just to let it be.

At times, the old man felt guilty about how he had acquired the memento. It had not come to him in an honorable way. But it was his now, and it would remain his until they pried it from his dead hand. He knew that, in life, people really don't own things; things own people until we lose them, toss them, sell them, give them away, or die. We spend time working to take care of things, protect them, only to lose them in the end. This birthstone keychain owned the old man for now; he guarded it and took it with him everywhere, as another once did. When he was gone, another would do the same. For now, though, his life was attached to the token; their purposes had become intertwined, and one was not complete without the other.

He could feel the warmth of the sun on his face as he caressed the stone in his hand. Happy times gone by filled his head and put a smile on his face. Although time had done much to wrinkle his face, the expression pushed away the frown lines for now. The stone had done its job, reinvigorating the old man with pleasant memories. He contentedly slid the keychain back into his pocket for safekeeping until it was needed again. To anyone other than the old man, the keychain would seem a cheap trifle, perhaps fetching fifty cents at a yard sale. To the old man, however, it was worth the world, and it *had* been his world for quite some time now, not that he had planned it that way.

But whose life was really planned out anyway? And when there was a plan, when did it work out as expected? The old man thought back to the businessmen scurrying through the park. We all have such great plans when we are young. Like those businessmen, the old man had planned to live a long life. He hadn't realized that he would be alone when his wish came true. He hadn't foreseen that all his friends, loved ones, and family would have gone, leaving him to sit alone in the park. He only had his keychain now. It was his one possession that seemed to sum up his life, and it had a permanent home tucked safely in his pocket.

He often wondered how something so small could mean so much to him. Maybe he just had a lot of his time invested in it. He had worked his whole life for so much more and so many other worldly things. But they were just things, things that break or go out of style. He had traded his life, his time on this earth, for money in order to buy them. Now, in his old age, he regretted all of those hours he had spent making money to buy things that were now meaningless to him. But the keychain hadn't cost him a dime, and it meant so much to him now. Maybe that's how life is, he mused. The things we obtain for free such as love, family, health, and friends tend to mean much more than things we spend our money on—cars, clothes, houses. When we're young, it seems like we have to have those things, that we can't live without them. But in the end, those *things* take our lives as payment. The old man pushed that depressing reflection from his mind to focus on happier times.

As he retreated into his memories, the old man felt someone touch him. He jumped at having his peace broken, but he also jumped as if his soul had been jolted. He had thought he was alone in his corner of the park. A strange feeling came over him and filled his body with emptiness. He thought he might know who the stranger was simply from the touch. He glanced into his periphery and saw someone standing next to him. Who was this, he wondered, and he turned his head abruptly to see who it was—a little too quickly for his age. He became light headed and waited for the disorientation to pass. As his eyes cleared, the man's face came into focus. *Larry*!

How did he find me again? He knew why Larry had found him, and he knew what Larry wanted. He had known Larry for way too many years to mistake him, but the young man he once knew was now in his forties, and clearly looked his age.

Larry was of an average height. He was of an average build. He was of average appearance. In fact, everything about Larry was eerily average, even normal. Despite all of his normality, there was something about him that made people, including the old man, feel that Larry was someone you really wouldn't want to spend much time with; not the kind of guy you would invite over to the house for dinner. There was nothing wrong with his appearance, but he somehow appeared—or, better yet, felt—*weird*. It's funny how some people are like that. You could dress Larry up in his best clothing, cut his hair, and splash the best smelling cologne on him. Nevertheless, Larry would still seem to be out of place no matter where he was. As his mother had always said, "You can dress them up, but you can't take them out. They just don't clean up." The old man had seen people like this trying so hard to be accepted, only to end up shunned by everyone. That was the way it was with Larry. He did all the right things and said all the right things, but something about him just made people stand away. *And here he is standing next to my bench, in my park, on my lovely afternoon*, the old man thought.

The old man didn't know what to say, but, not wanting to seem rude, he spoke up and said the first thing that came to his mind. "It's that time of year again," he began. "Soon winter will be here. Always comes after fall, you know. A lot like the seasons of life." The old man hoped to get the talking going. He knew you had two kind of basic conversations with people. The first type was talking *at* someone, the way a teacher or boss would inform their inferiors. The other person might interject with a question, but the conversation was clearly one sided. This was not the type of dialogue he wanted to have with Larry. He had done this in the past with him, and he knew it would ruin the effect of the beautiful afternoon. If he had to talk to Larry at all, the old man wanted to talk *with* Larry, to have a tete-a-tete, each listening and speaking in turn, exchanging ideas. That was the type of conversation the old man enjoyed, and he hoped Larry would take the cue.

The old man looked at Larry with a smile, hoping the young man would respond to the conversation starter. While waiting for Larry to say something, he realized that he had once again taken the stone out of his pocket during the awkward silence and was fumbling it through his hands resting on his lap. Although it was still in his hand, Larry could not see it. And the old man did not wish for Larry to see it. The young man might want it, and he was not ready for that yet. He careful let the keychain slip out of his hand and into his jacket pocket and avoided eye contact in hopes that Larry would not see it.

Larry said nothing. He just sat there, silent, thinking to himself. Despite the old man's sly movement, he had seen it out of the corner of his eye. In fact, the old man had missed slipping the rock into his pocket, and it was now lying on the ground at their feet. Larry eyed the keychain below the bench and realized that the old man didn't know it had slipped through his hands. *Good place for it now*, Larry thought to himself. The older man knew why Larry wanted the stone, or at least why he might want it. *He doesn't need it any more. It needs a new owner to take care of it.* Finally Larry asked the man on the bench, "May I sit?" As he spoke these words, a rather hefty breeze seemed to push the words off Larry's lips and deliver them to the old man. The falling leaves behind them danced up off the ground and waltzed by the both of them, some of them covering up the stone keychain under the park bench. Larry saw this but said nothing.

The old man was taken aback by the breeze; it almost took his breath out of him. After all, it came out of nowhere on a relatively a calm fall day. It was as if it started up just behind Larry and died after passing by him. It might have been just the fall wind winding up for winter, practicing for the winter winds, like a dust devil. As a kid the old man had seen dust devils kicking up on the hot summer Midwest prairie, taking a small cat or child for a short ride. Nevertheless, this breeze—or whatever it was—seemed to take his breath away. With no breath to speak, he simply patted the seat next to him and motioned for Larry to sit down.

As he regained his breath, he spoke softly. "Please sit. We meet again, I see."

In his mind, however, he thought, *I hope he doesn't take forever to answer me. Hopefully he will just tell me what he wants this time and move.*

But this time Larry responded quickly. "Yes. Yes we do."

The old man was surprised that Larry had answered so quickly and felt inclined to return in kind. "Not much time left on my old ticker. But there is always time for a familiar face. Aren't too many familiar faces left at my age."

Larry knew that the old man was referencing his age to incite pity, in hopes that Larry would not do what he had to do.

"In the past," the young man said, "you didn't always have a welcome mat laid out when you saw my face."

"Yes, yes," said the old man, nodding in agreement. "At my age, you don't have many choices of familiar faces, but there I go complaining again. I'm blessed to still be alive, or just damn lucky! I wanted to grow old, that was then I thought that I could keep a young body. If I was sixteen again and woke up in the body I have now, I would have thought that I was dying." The pair smiled at each other, breaking the ice. "Anyway," the old man continued, "let's talk about something else, shall we? Something that will be enjoyable for both of us."

Larry merely lowered his head and looked at the ground. Talking was not what Larry intended to do. He hadn't searched the old man out to have a friendly conversation. He had other tasks to do, and talking was not one of them. Although Larry hadn't planned on a chat, he realized that he had much to share. The day was so nice, and the bench was so comfortable. He had known the old man for a long time, but never really talked to him. Why not now? He searched for something to say to the old man, but nothing came to mind. The two sat in silence until Larry finally asked, "What would you like to talk about? I'm a great listener, but not much of a talker." He paused, adding, "I don't get much time for dialogue in my line of work."

The old man smiled in agreement. To himself, however, he added, *Hmmm. That is true. You can't be much of a talker when you're so damn boring.*

When Larry was speaking, most people would either walk away or drift off thinking about something else and act like they were listening. But Larry was here for something else, and the old man knew he needed to be on his toes. Nevertheless, Larry had searched him out for a reason. Given that the old man didn't have any pressing plans, he decided to sit and talk with Larry. Besides, he wanted to stall the young man a little longer.

"I'm sure you have a great talker in you," the old man replied. "Just like new and never been used. So, let's put some miles on it, shall we? We can start with the basics. Tell me a little about yourself. I have known you for years, but I really don't know much about you. Tell me the simple things. Like, what do you do for fun? That's always a nice way to start and keep a conversation going. Talk about something nice or about something you enjoy. The trick is that it has to be something that the other person can enjoy as well. "

The old man knew it was best for him to suggest topics. Otherwise, Larry might choose to talk about why he was really there. The old man wanted to avoid the elephant in the corner. Any topic was better than *that*.

Larry was caught off guard by the older man's willingness to talk to him now. Not many people had asked him about himself. When they did speak to him, they typically asked other questions. This was something new. He didn't have a script prepared for his response, and Larry prided himself on having a prepared answer for the questions he was asked most often. He had spent a lot of time coming up with answers for almost any question he might be faced with. He also had a list of general questions that would cover almost anything asked of him. If one of his scripted questions was asked, he had an answer ready to come out of his mouth without even thinking about it. He was also proud of the fact that he made sure his answers didn't offend anyone. His wife once told him his "scripts" made him sound boring, but he didn't believe it. He thought they made him sound more like a finely tuned instrument, precise and able to hit the right key at the right time. How could that be boring? It was a work of art to him.

For the first time in years, Larry began to speak off-script. *It won't matter in a few minutes from now anyway*, he said to himself. For now, he decided to open up and dump whatever came into his head. He looked around and actually noticed what the old man had been observing all morning. "I love the smells of fall," he began, "the leaves, the spices, crispness in the air. Mostly, though, I love the smell of lighted candles burning the top of jack-o-lanterns on a chilly Halloween night. Today reminds of one of those days." Larry's face began to light up, as if he could smell the candles now. "Halloween jack-o-lanterns are the best smelling things in the world. Nothing else comes close."

Larry had always thought it was a wonderful smell, quite possibly because it brought back good memories. It was the night he could pretend to be someone else.

"On Halloween night," he continued, "I could be special. I could be anybody. Anybody but me. Or maybe it was not being someone else. Maybe I hoped that that the someone else I could be would be someone normal." Larry broke eye contact from his bench buddy and lowered his head to the ground. As with many of his good memories, this one had been chased away by a bad memory. Why couldn't he let those good memories find a permanent home in his mind? The bad ones always seemed to flush them out, bringing in even more depressing thoughts to fill the empty space. But, sitting with the old man on the bench, Larry realized that some spirit of the good times remained in his soul. Talking about his past had brought it out from the depths. On Halloween he could be normal. Maybe he didn't have to be the weird kid with no dad around. Maybe he didn't have to be the kid who was teased mercilessly for his special reading glasses. Maybe he didn't have to be the kids with dyslexia. Maybe he didn't have to be the strange kid that no one wanted to talk to in school. He could just be normal, or, better yet, above normal. Thinking aloud, Larry added, "Maybe the smell of jack-o-lanterns gave me hope to be normal someday. The other kids dressed up like Superman, or Batman, or Spiderman—superheroes. I just hoped I could be normal." Through all this, Larry never raised his eyes off the ground.

"Hope is all we have Larry," echoed the old man. "Hope is a funny word. It's a word so small, but astonishingly powerful. I have seen so much done in the illusion of hope: the hope of a better life, the hope of a better place, the hope of safety, the hope of love, the hope of becoming a better person. And your hope of being normal or liked by others is common. I often wonder how one little word can hold so much power." He stopped, waiting for Larry to look him in the eyes. When this didn't happen, he continued, "Hope is all you have going for you until you meet your goals. Hope is what it takes to get you there someday." The old man stopped again, noticing that Larry was looking him in the eyes now and listening intently to what he was saying.

The old man decided to push on. "Too many people have the power of taking away hope in others, to crush it in someone else. The question is, how do you *give* hope to someone else? You can take it easily, but it's not so easy to give away. In my lifetime, I've learned that hope can make or break someone. We almost need it as much as we need love, if not more. If you don't have the hope of being loved, how can you love someone? Everyone needs hope, and then we learn to use our gifts and special talents to help others. We can be inspired by the hope others gave us. Because of that, that makes us all special in some way. Don't you think, Larry? Our hopes, when mixed with our special talents, make us different from each other."

Larry was taken aback at the word "special." He enjoyed what the old man was saying, but his use of that word made him cringe. "Special" was not a good word to Larry. It had never been used as a positive word in reference to himself before. In school, "special ed" was not a good thing. His classmates let him know that. There are some words in life that create positive images, but others can burn a hole through your soul. For Larry, that word was "special."

He knew the old man was using the word in a positive way, though. Larry thought back to his second grade teacher. He started remembering when sitting in the classroom and what life was like back then—the smell of chalk, the alphabet running across the top of the board, the sound of his classmates' laughter, the bell signaling lunch time. And he remembered his teacher, Mrs. Smith. "Everybody has a special talent," she told them. "You just need to figure out what that special talent is." Mrs. Smith was so nice to him, not like the others who merely put him in the back. They seemed to blame him for his special needs. So, Larry and those teachers had made a silent agreement: they would pass Larry along, ignoring him completely, if he wouldn't make any noise or act out during class. So, because of this unwritten contract, Larry remained silent, never asked questions, never asked for extra help, and never interacted with his peers. Mrs. Smith, though, was different. She wanted him to ask questions and learn new things. She wanted to give him all the help he needed. She treated him as an equal to the other kids, never distinguishing her favorites by the grade they received or how quickly someone learned the information.

Larry wondered if he should share this thought with his bench mate. He was not sure that the old man would understand. However, since the man had finished talking, Larry decided that it was his turn to talk. "I had one teacher that always said that everyone is good at something. I always thought she just told me that to make me feel better about myself. At the time, the only hope I had was of seeing my father again someday. That does not make you special. I did not know my dad, and my mom told me very little about him. I only had an old birthstone keychain that was his. I believe you know of it."

The old man froze, waiting to see if Larry would ask for it. He was sure that Larry knew he had it now. He knew that Larry was here for something else, but maybe he was also here to get the keychain stone back. The old man started to say something, but, before he could, Larry spoke again.

"He left that keychain behind when he went away. Not much else. But then he really didn't have much, I suppose. My mom gave it to me when I got older. She tossed everything else when we got kicked out of our house for late payments. The keychain was a sign of my hope of seeing my dad some day. Hope that he would come back and save us. Hope that he had some good reason for running out on us. Hope that he would change his mind. But, as you know, the stone became a sign of other things."

Larry had not seen the old birthstone keychain in some time. He had forgotten about it until he saw it fall under the park bench today. Larry briefly thought, *No matter. It had lost all the hope it gave to me when I was younger. It needs find its new owner now.* As a child, he dreamed that his dad was someone important. In his mind, his father had only left because he couldn't be with his family, not because he didn't want to be with his family. He felt stupid now having believed that as a kid. How wrong he had been. But, as a child, you are filled with hope until it's pulled out of you part by part. Like a wad of gum stuck in a mess of hair, slowly being pulled out strand by strand until there was nothing left. Over time, life seems to drain hope from you.

Larry realized that sometimes it's best not to know the truth. Sometimes we don't want to find out the truth behind the lies. He had a co-worker who bought a lottery ticket three times a year. He wouldn't check the numbers for months. He preferred to live with the hope that he won, and could quit his job. When he finally did check the numbers, his hope was extinguished, and he became just another loser again. Why take hope away from yourself each week or day when you can keep that hope alive for months?

The old man could tell that Larry was deep in thought by the way he quietly sat beside him on the bench. Larry's face was full of movement as thoughts of times gone by bounced around in his mind. Those thoughts wanted to be heard, but Larry wouldn't let them out. Why did he wait so long to ask these questions? He decided it was time to get Larry back into the conversation.

"Do you remember the first time we met?" the old man asked abruptly. "I was a cop then. I could tell the first day we met you didn't have a good home life or a father figure around.

Larry cut him off, not rudely but wanting to add to the topic. "You were right. I didn't have a father figure. I tried to find someone. For a while, there was an older man who lived next to us: Mr. Jamison. He was like a dad to me; he took me on walks and got me involved in the church. I thought he was a good man. Maybe too good. The Jamisons tried to help out a man recently released from prison. They let him stay with them and tried to find him a job. But when my mom found out that the man was imprisoned for pedophilia, my mom wouldn't let me go to the Jamison's house anymore. I wasn't even allowed to talk to Mr. Jamison. I'm not sure why you would put someone who had just gotten out of jail in a neighborhood full of kids. Seems like letting an alcoholic live next to a bar. Anyway, Mr. Jamison was just another father figure who fell out of my life. I've got many stories like that. Too many." Larry grew silent for another minute before addressing the old man again. "How did you know that I didn't have a father figure back then?"

"A bad home life leads to troubled kids, eighty percent of the time. As a cop, when I saw a fatherless kid, I made it a point to check in on them and make sure they stayed out of trouble. That's when I took notice of you, Larry. Do you remember that day?"

"I remember you giving me a look that said, 'I'll be watching you.'"

"Is that all you remember about that day?"

As much as he wanted to, Larry could never forget that day. Up to that point, his life had been fairly normal. He had friends he could run around with. But that day changed everything. If he could go back and change one day in his past, that would have been the one. His life seemed so good back then before the events of that day.

On that day, both of their lives had clashed and the two became entangled for the rest of their lives. That was part of the reason Larry was here today. He had hunted down the old man in order to set the record straight. He wanted to explain his side of the story, as an adult rather than a kid trying to protect himself. Now was the time to tell his story.

Chapter Two
In the Heat of Summer

It was a hot summer when the two first met each other. School was out for the year, and Larry was not enrolled in his "special" reading class. He had brought up his reading grade and had tested out of the summer program—just by the skin of his teeth. That summer started out wonderfully. There was no reason for the other children to make fun of him. Instead, he had plenty of time to run around and play. He was able to make friends and fit in with the other children. He was still the same weird, poor kid from the wrong side of the tracks, but he had friends that were the same, so all was well. He was happy, enjoying life in the way that only kids who blend in with their peers can. Walking by yourself made you stand out, made you an easy target for the bullies. There was safety in numbers, and Larry took advantage of that ideal as the summer began. He never understood why the phrase, "Stand up and be counted," was seen as a positive statement about asserting your individuality. Actually, it seemed the complete opposite to Larry. He didn't want to stand up or stick out; he just wanted to blend into the woodwork. Part of his understanding was probably based on overhearing his mother talk about her boss, who claimed that, "If I don't know your name at the end of the day, you did a good job. I want your opinion, I'll tell it to you. So let's cut out the middleman—you—and don't tell me any opinions."

His school system also taught Larry the benefits of blending in to the crowd. The teachers actively prepared their students for a life of mass marketing and production. Wear what everyone else is wearing. Do what everyone else is doing. Buy what everyone else is buying, and buy a lot of it. Work from eight to five. Then buy some more. Blend in. Don't be different. Be normal, or you'll get teased and harassed by others. Larry realized later in life that the educational system had been started and sold to large companies as a place to train people to be better workers, more agreeable workers, more passive, mindless workers. Until the modern school system was setup, many of children worked in the plants. Powerful companies did not want to give up their cheap labor, but agreed to support a mandatory school system, if it would lead to more productive workers in the end. So the schools did their best to train the kids to blend in, to arrive promptly at eight, to be attentive, to absorb information at face value, to fight amongst themselves for the good of the company. And the students quickly learned that a swift punishment would be the reward for not following the rules. Larry learned that quickly as well, but he had a harder time appearing to fit in.

But the rules had disappeared now that school was out. He and his friends could make up their own rules to the games they played throughout the day.

The day that Larry first met the old man was a scorcher. Steamy vapor waves slowly rose from the pavement, sucking every bit of water from the tiny pores in the cement. Larry and his friends were looking for some way to cool off and get out of the sun. They decided that a trip to the nearby lake would take the edge off of the day's oppressive heat. None of their folks belonged to the high-end country club, which had its own pool, and the public pool had been shut down to save money, mostly owing to the fact that the board members were also members of the country club. So the lake became the getaway for the underprivileged children like Larry and his friends. But that wasn't a problem. They would never run into any of the rich kids there.

Even though the lake was green, had a thickish consistency, and was overgrown with weeds for the first three feet, it seemed a paradise to the sweaty children. Since the shoreline was not landscaped, they couldn't walk into the water without being attacked by hoards of leeches and mosquitoes. But the children had found a way to avoid all that by jumping off a broken-down dock and staying away from the sides. This also allowed them to steer clear of the empty beer cans, cigarette butts, and occasional water moccasins that lapped up beside the shore.

Sam, Joe, Mike, and Tim gathered outside Larry's house, which was nicely poised in the center of the rundown neighborhood. Even though his mom wouldn't let him have anybody inside when she was away at work for the day, the group used the front lawn as a meeting point. When they had assembled, Larry hopped on his bike and sped away towards the cool lake water, his friends following closely behind. The bike represented freedom to Larry. It was a green monkey bike, from back in the day before ten speeders, but he considered himself lucky to have it. Before his mom had had her accident at work, they hadn't been able to afford a bike, so Larry had to walk around, watching his friends practice new maneuvers and pop wheelies around the neighborhood. Now that he had one of his own, he could blend into the group more easily.

And he cherished his bike. Each time he put even a small mark on it, his mother reminded him that she didn't plan on getting hurt again to buy him another one. So Larry took extra good care of the bike, both out of fear that he wouldn't get another and out of respect for his mother and her sacrifices. Thinking back now, Larry wished she wouldn't have bought that for him. He was always scared of losing it or of doing something to the bike because of what she said. When he was a little kid, someone told him, "If you step on a crack, you break your mother's back." For months, he was petrified that he might accidentally step on a crack and paid painstakingly close attention to where he walked. He had the same feeling about the bike. He had only one parent, and he could not lose her.

The black bike seat had risen to near blistering levels from its stint in the front yard that morning, so Larry had to stand on the pedals as he coasted down the street to keep the plastic from melting into his backside. On the way back from the lake, it would not be a problem, because his swimming suit would be wet and that would cool the hot seat. Larry didn't mind standing as he rode, since most of the ride to the lake was downhill. The boys took full advantage of the wind on their faces, pedaling as fast as they could and leaning down over the handlebars to become more aerodynamic to build speed as they raced down the hill. They took turns as one pulled in front of the other on their race to the lake. Soon, though, Larry began to fall behind. Since he had to stand up on the pedals for most of the ride, he couldn't go as fast as the other boys could.

Larry pumped his legs as hard as they would go, fruitlessly trying to keep up with the others.

His friends let up a bit, so Larry was able to catch up. As he pulled closer, a strange smell wafted back to him. Someone smelled really bad. It was Sam.

Sam was a nice kid. He came from a very large family, so everything he owned had, at one time or another, been someone else's. Sam's bike was a hand-me-down; his clothing was hand-me-down; his room was a hand-me-down. But Sam did the best he could with what he had. He was a cheerful kid and fun to be around.

Today, though, a pungent odor was wafting off Sam, made even more pronounced by the wafting of the wind made by the riders. Larry couldn't take it, and pulled behind one of the other boys as they raced down the hill to the lake. Sam looked over and saw Larry making a face at being downwind of him. He couldn't hide his distaste, and Sam was the first to notice.

"Larry, what's up? You're freaking me out with that weird look you're giving me," Sam said.

Without thinking, Larry stated the truth. "You smell, man! I can hardly be downwind of you! I thought you stank yesterday, but it's worse today! Take a bath or something!" As the words poured out of his mouth thoughtlessly, Larry immediately wished he could take them back. He knew Sam came from a large, poor family. Likely, he could only take one shower per week.

Larry looked around at the other boys. They were giving him dirty looks, looks that screamed, "Shut up right now! You crossed the line." Larry bit his lip and gave Sam an apologetic smile.

Sam smiled back. It was the code of the group. They all had been picked on at some point or another. That was one of the things that made them all friends. In school, they were all in a special reading group. But Larry and his friends were the "star pupils" of that group, and all of the other kids in the class wanted to be friends with them. In any other classroom, they didn't have the same respect or same social standing, but, when they were together, they were a strong force. Larry knew better than to push the issue. He didn't want to be outside of the group again.

"Larry, quit messing with us and quit with 'the smell thing' again, maybe you stink," Mike yelled.

Larry had talked to the boys about his ability to smell things others couldn't, but it didn't go over very well with them. In fact, it didn't go over at all. It fell on deaf ears and almost cost him his spot in the group. He already knew that they were looking to replace him with another kid who had just moved into town. The new kid's mom gave them ice cream and let them come into the house, unlike Larry's mom. Had they agreed to go over to the new kid's house today, instead of meeting up with Larry, each of boys would have gotten an ice cream cone already. Instead, they were listening to Larry drone on about Sam smelling badly. Even though the new kid's father was the new city undertaker and his house was doubled as the mortuary, Larry knew he was on thin ice. His friends might "upgrade" him for an endless supply of ice cream cones, even if there were dead bodies in the basement.

"Guys," shouted Tim, who was known as the peacemaker of the group. "We're going swimming, so that should knock the stink off of all of us. Cure it or kill it, I always say!" The boys all laughed and the tension seemed to diminish.

Tim had a gift for lightening up the conversation from time to time. In his household, he had two older sisters. During family arguments, one sister would side with his dad and the other with his mom. Tim was always in the middle. Sometimes even a stupid little argument would go on for days. Much of the time during the holidays—a time that should've been good family time—just seemed to go bad. Tim's family would ask him to pick a side, and that was always a bad move. The losing side would punish him and not talk to him for days. So Tim learned to joke and make them all laugh in order to stay neutral. He did this with his friends, too, and the group liked being around him more than Larry. Tim saw the other boys starting to get upset with Larry and did what he did best: make them laugh and joke about it.

Larry was glad for the reprieve. Even though he decided it was best to keep his thoughts to himself, Larry still shied away from Sam. The smell had gotten so pungent that Larry had to stifle a gag. He had smelled that odor before, but when?

It was his granddad. His granddad was one of the few men in his life that spent any time with him. He cherished the times he had spent with his granddad. At a certain point, though, his granddad had developed that smell. Larry hated the fact that he cared so much for his granddad, but could hardly be in the room with him. The smell had actually caused him to get sick on a few occasions. It started out small but grew and grew. Finally, Larry made lame excuses to his mother about why he couldn't go to granddad's house anymore. Now that his granddad had passed away, Larry regretted not going with his mother to see him more often. He hadn't even said goodbye in the end. His mom thought his granddad died of a broken heart because Larry wouldn't spend more time with him.

"He smells like my granddad," Larry thought. Unfortunately, he also said it out loud.

He needed to really think about what to say next time. He thought about coming up with a set of scripts—a proper statement for every occasion. He would need a list of self preapproved comments that would sound appropriate and could be used at any moment.

His friends all stopped riding and stared at him. He had definitely crossed the line. Even Tim was clearly shocked by the rude, stupid remark. But Larry looked at him, pleading with his eyes for Tim to issue another one-liner to break the tension and move the focus on to a new topic. Tim sighed, but acquiesced. "Then maybe Sam should get together with him and have a stink fest! They could play a game and have prizes. They could have a whole day of fun for all of us."

All the boys began to laugh. But Larry wasn't laughing. Tim realized that he had hit a sour spot with Larry and hurt him.

Larry thought about his granddad and how much he really missed him. He remembered how much he wanted him back in his life. The pain of his passing filled him and he spoke again without thinking. He spoke from his heart.

"My granddad passed away last year."

None of the boys had any reaction. How can you react to that? Instead, they pretended that they didn't hear Larry. It was sad about his granddad's passing, but luckily they had reached the lake, so they could drop the topic.

They reached the lake and dumped their bikes on the dry, sun toasted grass. The town was in the middle of a heat spell and most un-watered lawns had burned up. The city had just mown this part of the park, and the grass was dead from the summer heat. Even the lake had gone down some, partly from the heat and partly from the fact that the country club used the lake to water their golf courses and yards.

The boys sped off for the dock, anticipating the cool rush of hitting the water. Larry knew if he brought up Sam's smell again, he would be dunked under water as soon he had gotten in. *How is it that no one else can smell him?* Larry fell behind the others as they ran toward the water. Even worse, the odor made his thoughts continually turn back to his granddad. More than others, it seemed, Larry had an acute sense of smell. Smells brought back vivid memories for the young boy in ways that they didn't seem to affect others.

The smell of hot apple pie was another trigger for Larry. When he was visiting his granddad, his grandma would often make apple pie, knowing it was his favorite. While he and his granddad would tinker in the garage, the aromatic waves would waft from the kitchen window, as if seeking out Larry's nose. Not only did the smell remind him of his grandma's pies, but they reminded hum of the joys he experienced with his grandparents. Years later, if Larry was in town and happened to walk by a bakery, he would instantly recall those happy days from his past. In his mind, he would be standing in his grandma's kitchen, watching her carefully select the perfect apples for his dessert.

As much as the smell of apple pie brought forth joyous memories, the smell coming off of Sam now made Larry shudder in remembrance of the way he had treated his granddad.

Larry tried to shake the thought from his mind, now. It was time to have fun, and Larry wanted to cool off with his friends. The other boys were in an all-out sprint to the dock, each vying to be the first to jump into the water. Larry knew that, even though he had fallen behind, he was the fastest runner of the group and could have easily taken them all. In fact, Larry was the fastest runner at their school. He had tried out for the school's track team, and beat out one of the country-club boys for the school record. Rather than helping him become more popular, though, the race had rendered him even more of an outcast. The jocks beat him up after school for his win. Apparently, they didn't like the fact that someone from the "special" reading class was a faster runner than their champion. They waited outside for him in a similar fashion after every single track practice. Eventually, he quit the team. He enjoyed track, but not getting beat up.

Instead of sprinting past his friends, Larry noticed that Sam was in the lead. He decided to lag behind in an attempt to make up for his earlier rude comments. To stall a little more, Larry took the towel from around his neck and laid it on the ground. Quickly, he pulled out the lucky keychain his dad had left behind and rubbed it with his fingers, his ritual whenever felt out of place or stressed. The keychain with a dark blue stone was very special to him, and just touching it soothed him. He set it carefully in the middle of his towel, folded the towel in half to keep the charm in place, and took off running after the others.

Tim, Joe, Mike, and Sam were all nearing the end of the dock, shoving past one another as quickly as they could towards the end and the water. Sam had kept a marginal lead.

When he reached the edge, he did a flying head-first dive into the water to win the race. It was a great dive. He had jumped into the air like a swan, anticipating how great the water was going to feel. It was a great dive, one for the records, one to put in the books. It was also his last dive.

As the other boys reached the end, they dove into the water as well, but none as spectacularly as Sam had. They rose to the surface in a ruckus, ready to congratulate Sam on his success. It wasn't until Joe started screaming that they knew something was wrong. Joe lifted his hand out of the water, and blood came pouring down his arm.

"What happened," Mike yelled, swimming over to Joe.

"I hit my hand on something," Joe cried.

Tim dunked back under the water to search for the culprit. He reappeared a few seconds later. "Some idiot drove a golf cart into the lake," he informed the other boys.

"A golf cart?" Mike asked incredulously. "Sounds like the good for nothing country clubbers probably raided their parents' liquor cabinets last night."

The boys investigated, and, sure enough, about two inches under the surface was the roof of a big, white golf cart. They hadn't seen it from the shoreline because the water was too green and cloudy.

"Hey," Tim said, "where's Sam?"

In their clamor over Joe's hand and the submerged golf, none of them had realized that Sam was missing. They scanned the surface of the water. Then they began to scream.

Sam was floating face down in the water a few yards from the rest of them. Larry jumped into the water straight away, furiously paddling toward his friend. Mike was right behind him. Sam wasn't moving. Each of the boys put one of Sam's limp arms around their neck and towed him back to the dock.

Tim and Joe had climbed back onto the dock and lifted Sam out of the water, laying him carefully on his back. Mike ran off for help while the others examined Sam's body. Blood was seeping from the top of his head, where a deep gash was embedded below his hair.

"He's not breathing!" Tim noted.

Joe began to scream for help.

Larry just stood there in disbelief. His mind was in shock, and his body was numb.

It seemed like hours before Mike came back with help. Larry was still silently standing over Sam while the other two were sobbing on the ground next to the lifeless body. The police officer pushed the boys out of the way so he could examine Sam.

An ambulance blared in the background, but Larry's world had gone fuzzy as if he was looking at the world reflected in a funhouse mirror. He didn't even see the punch until it was inches away from his face.

The force knocked Larry to the ground. He looked up and saw Mike standing over him. His eyes were shooting daggers, and his fists were still clenched.

"What the hell, Mike?" Tim yelled. "What did you do that for?" He put himself between the two.

Joe helped Larry to his feet. Tim had to hold Mike back from resuming his attack.

"You told him he stunk, man! You treated him like trash, and now he's dead!" Tears were streaming from Mike's eyes.

Larry remained mute. It was true.

"You were on the dock," Mike continued his harangue. "You should have seen him! You should have told us, you freak! If you had just told us, maybe we could have saved him! If you hadn't been thinking about that imaginary smell, maybe you would have seen! Maybe he wouldn't be dead! It's your fault!"

Larry didn't know how to respond. All three were looking at him now. Did they really think it was his fault?

"You've always been a freak! You were jealous of Sam! You knew we liked him better. You're probably happy he's dead!"

Tears burned in Larry's eyes. Was Mike right? Of course, he had always known he was on the outside of their group. Sure, he was jealous of Sam. Jealous of the way Sam seemed to fit in everywhere he went. Jealous of the way the others treated him. But that didn't mean he wanted him dead!

"Mike…" Larry began timidly, taking a step forward.

Mike shoved him back. "Get away from me, freak! You're a crappy friend. Get away from us all."

Larry picked himself off the ground again. He looked at Tim. He knew that Mike was just overreacting. Certainly Tim didn't think he wanted Sam dead. But Tim just lowered his eyes, and Joe avoided his gaze altogether.

So that's how it's going to be? They all knew what it felt like to be on the outside. As such, they all knew better than to voice their opinions against Mike. It would be social suicide—at least from their small social circle.

Larry shook his head and retreated back to the bikes. He sat down on his towel and thumbed his keychain.

The next few hours were a blur. Dozens of police officers, and EMTs, and firefighters, and curious passersby came and went. The boys were asked the same questions over and over again. When the new kid's dad showed up, Larry knew it was over.

His mom put her arm around him. "C'mon, honey," she said softly, urging him up the hill and away from the scene.

Larry shot a final glance back to the other boys who were talking to the police officer that Mike had found. He was met with icy stares. He turned and let his mother guide him home.

Chapter Three
It Made Sense Now

The old man sat silently as Larry finished telling the story. A watery sun broke through the puffy clouds that were hovering in the sky. Both looked in the direction of the lake where Sam had died. That spot had been sold to a company who put up some office buildings. They drained the lake and built over it.

It didn't really matter, though, since the city posted a no swimming notice after Sam's death, ruling the area unsafe for children. They had been scared of a lawsuit. None of the country club boys who drove the cart into the lake got charged with anything. Of course, it always helped to have your dad on the city council in those sorts of situations.

The two sat mutely. The old man gave Larry some time to grieve about that day. To grieve the loss of Sam. And to grieve the loss of his childhood friends.

He knew that the boys had nothing more to do with Larry after the accident. He had taken it upon himself to keep an eye on the boys after that day, especially Larry, whose behavior had puzzled him. He had overheard Mike yelling that Sam's death was Larry's fault. He had seen how his friends avoided him from then on. But, until now, he had never known why.

It made sense now. The boys felt guilty for letting Sam win the race to the lake. They thought it was Larry's fault that he had died. If he hadn't been teasing Sam so mercilessly, someone else would have jumped in first and Sam would still be alive. It was childish logic. Larry had been rude and upset Sam, so they let Sam go ahead of them to compensate. Sam had died because of that; therefore it was Larry's fault. And not only that, but Larry made fun of him just minutes before he died. In a child's mind, that is something you can't forgive. The old man finally understood Larry's pain.

He had been on police escort for Sam's
funeral and saw Mike accost Larry outside of
the church. Larry had gone to the funeral by
himself; his mom couldn't get the day off work.
He had been standing outside when the others
boys walked up. Mike yelled at Larry, as tears
streamed down his face. "It was his fault. It was
all *his* fault," he cried, pointing to Larry.
Mike's dad guided him inside before he could
cause a scene. The cop watched as Larry slowly
became the only person standing outside by
himself, not sure whether he should enter the
church. Larry had looked at him sadly, then
slowly turned and walked home. He knew he
was not welcomed.

After that Officer The cop never saw
Larry with the group anymore; he was always
by himself. The cop had known all too well that
now Larry's chances of getting into to trouble
grew, being an outsider. With all of the media
attention on school shootings and bullying, the
police force required all officers to take a

training course that trained them how to spot potentially trouble youths. He needed to watch Larry. But, after hearing Larry's story, the old man now realized that the day at the lake had been a major turning point in the young man's life, something that would shape him forever.

The old man could see that Larry was stuck for words and didn't know what else to say now. He thought it was time to respond to the story, so he added, "I tried to save his life, but the boy was dead. You just stood over him, obviously in shock."

Larry sighed, hesitant to continue his narrative. He wished he had one of his predefined scripts—something light and noncommittal. But he chose to speak from the heart.

Chapter Four
Schools Out, Lesson Learned

Larry was happy that the final bell had rung for the day. He hated school even more now. Not only did he have to deal with the country club kids teasing him about his dyslexia, but Mike and his gang had made sure that everyone knew about his little incident in Paul's basement. Even though he had to walk home alone, Larry felt a weight lifted off of his shoulders when he left the building.

As he entered the dining room, he saw his mom sitting at the table in the kitchen having coffee with some of her friends. Larry liked coming home to having his mom there. He especially liked it when his mom had friends over for afternoon coffee. There would always be cookies on the table, and he knew he could have some—his mother would not stop him from taking one in front of the other ladies. He also liked that his mom wasn't alone. She had friends. People to chat with.

On this particular day, they were too busy talking about who did what to whom to notice Larry. In reality, the only time they really talked to him was to pump information out of him about someone he might know. It amazed him how the women could just gab about other people for hours. Their sentences always seemed to start with "did you hear…" or "I heard…" and sometimes, "I bet…" The conversation always seemed to be about other people that were not in the room. Sometimes he would hang out in the next room and listen to what they were talking about. He would laugh out loud at the wild claims they were making, claims that in no way could be true. Unfortunately, Larry knew just how quickly the truth could change when it was repeated throughout the town. By the end of the day, the lies had been repeated so many times that it became a fact in the small minds of the townspeople.

But Larry really didn't care who they talked about, as long as it wasn't him. He had been on the losing end of mindless gossip too much since school started up again.

Larry decided to stay out of their way today. He quietly crept into the dining room, stepping in between two very round women to grab a cookie from the table before retreating to his room. But as he did, the odor infiltrated his nasal passages. One of the ladies reeked of death. It was overwhelmingly strong, almost as bad as Paul's basement. Before he knew what he was doing, he gasped loudly and pulled back, his eyes watering from the smell.

Apparently, they were watering so badly that it looked as though he was crying. He couldn't hide it—especially not from this hyper-observant group. He backed away, trying his best not to get sick from the smell. All he needed was to puke on one of his mother's friends. He'd never hear the end of it. The schoolboy expression, "lose your cookies," seemed all too real at this particular moment. He wanted to giggle at the thought, but he knew that, if he did, he would retch everywhere.

When he was a safe distance from the woman and the odor—far enough to where he could actually breathe easily again—he saw the group had turned to stare at him. He made eye contact with the woman. This wasn't good. Instantly, she could see he was repulsed by her. Her face grew bright red, a perfect mixture of anger and embarrassment. She was aware that she was overweight, but Larry had made it worse by insinuating that she stank as well.

Larry quickly removed himself, retreating to the hallway. The group turned to look at Larry's mother, as if she had just received the worst parent of the year award. She got up from the table, obviously agitated.

She rushed out, grabbing his shoulders and holding him in place. Larry knew that the women could hear her. "What's wrong with you Larry?" she growled at him as she shook his body like a rag doll.

Larry knew that she wasn't going to let him go until he gave her a satisfactory answer. Unfortunately, he hadn't come up with any of his scripts yet. Instead, he opted for the truth.

"Mom, she has that smell on her...that smell of death." He tried to whisper so that they other women wouldn't hear. He didn't want to embarrass her in front of her friends any more than he already had. Since his dad had left, many of her friends had abandoned her. Larry knew, more than anybody, what it was like to feel ostracized. He didn't want that for his mother as well. She deserved better. And, if this gaggle of women heard him, the story would be all over town by nightfall.

"What are you saying? That crap again? Stop it! Stop it, Larry!" she hissed, in a much louder tone this time.

The women in the next room had had risen and circled around the woman Larry had embarrassed. They were clearly telling her that she was all right, that nothing was wrong with her, that Larry was just a very rude kid.

He overheard one of them. "It's Larry. He's a weird kid. You shouldn't listen to him!"

Larry already knew that many of the women talked badly about him to the others in town. They said things that shouldn't have been said. The round woman who smelled badly was the worst of the bunch. Her daughter was one of the more popular kids at school. And she'd repeat whatever her mom had told her all around school. Many of times in front of Larry.

His mom gripped his shoulders even harder now, forcing Larry to look into her eyes. She pulled him closer to her and ordered, "Go to your room! Get out of here, and stop talking about that stupid smell and all this death crap." The words "death crap" bounced off the walls and entered the room full of coffee hens. As it hit their ears, Larry could almost see their faces light up with hate and disbelief. Even Larry's mom stopped in her tracks, wishing she hadn't said anything. She pushed Larry aside and headed back into the dining room. Cleary she was on damage control.

By now, Larry thought that his mom's idea of him going to his room was an excellent one. Besides, the smell of death was now filling up the hallway. It was definitely time to leave. He pulled his keychain from his pocket and started to play with it as he did in times of stress. With all of the torments he had undergone lately, he didn't even realize that he was doing it anymore. It had just become a habit. It was instinctive.

As he started to walk away, out of the corner of his eye he saw the robust, stinky, mean woman fall over to the floor, hitting her head hard on the table as she went down. The sound reminded Larry of a watermelon being cracked open. At first, Larry was pleased. *Maybe it will knock some sense into her.* But he also knew he was never going to hear the end of this. He knew the other hens in the room would blame him for being rude instead of blaming her for being overly dramatic.

He hesitantly followed his Mom, who had rushed back into the room. Although he knew he was walking into a verbally abusive situation, he also knew that if he didn't help his mother he would be in for an earful anyway.

One of the ladies jumped up and grabbed the phone. She dialed 911 and asked for help. Larry thought this was going a little too far, as the woman was known for her "spells." She had problems in the past, passing out in inappropriate. In fact, she had so many of them that most people didn't pay them much attention. They'd just make sure she was comfortable and wait for the spell to pass.

But he knew that this would spark a new line of gossip about him. He could hear them now. "We had to call 911. She fell after Larry made fun of her. It was just too much for her to take."

He stood back as the other women surrounded her body. They were all busy fussing over her—fanning her with magazines, loosening the top button of her dress, snapping their fingers in front of her face, and crying…lots and lots of crying.

Suddenly, his mom hit him on the back of the arm, somehow making it look like a hug to keep up appearances. He looked down and realized that the round woman was now dead a doornail. She was gone.

Just as Larry realized this, the front door swung open. It was the cop, the same cop who showed up when Sam hit his head on the golf cart in the lake. The same cop who he had met before under the same events. The cop seemed as surprised to see Larry as Larry was to see him.

"I was close by, so I made it here first," the officer said to the crying women. "I heard the call on my radio. The paramedics are on the way."

Larry wondered whether his appearance was just an unfortunate coincidence or if the man had been following him. It was a small town, but not so small that there was only one police officer.

The cop ushered the ladies back from the body and gestured for Larry and his Mom to stay away also. He looked at Larry, and it was obvious from his expression that he recognized him. The cop glanced down at the keychain in

Larry's hand and then back into his eyes. Larry moved back quickly, forgetting that he was still rubbing the keychain. He had hoped the cop wouldn't remember him from the lake and, if he stood in the background, hopefully the officer wouldn't remember him from this incident either. He wasn't sure why the cop always seemed to show up at these events and did not care to learn.

In reality, the cop had been driving down the street when the radio crackled. The women at Larry's house had called for medical assistance. Since he was right down the street anyway, he got on the radio and announced he'd be going there to be on site when the paramedics arrived. The chief had been giving everyone a hard time about helping the paramedics out on their calls when they never returned the favor. He didn't mind though. In his eyes, they only needed to return the favor once—when he really needed them. As a cop, he never knew when someone was going to take a stab at him or try to shoot him. The way he figured it, he didn't want to upset the people who might one day save his life.

Hopefully, they could also do something for the woman lying at his feet. He performed a cursory examination to see if there was anything he could do before the medical team showed up. She looked dead to him, but he was not going to say anything until he knew for sure. He didn't want to upset the other women in the room, as he knew they would go hysterical as soon as they heard the news. He decided to make it look like she had a chance of making it, even if he already knew there wasn't any hope for survival.

He fussed around with pulse-taking and "giving her space to breathe." Soon the paramedics arrived on scene. "Vitals" were swiftly taken. They loaded the obese woman's body on the stretcher and raced to the hospital. The paramedics knew she was dead, but they also hadn't wanted to upset the women. Instead they hinted that some medical miracle could revive her.

The cop had to take some notes for a report and paperwork. He asked questions of all the women, partly to make them all feel better and that someone carried about the situation.

"So ladies, did you notice anything strange about her today?"

He waited to hear someone say something like, "She said she wasn't feeling well" or even, "She said her underwear seemed tight today." However, what he heard that day shocked him, which was hard to do.

The women noted that Larry had been acting strangely around the victim right before she fell down. Maybe he had done something to her, slipped something in her coffee maybe. Maybe he had had something to do with her spell.

Larry remained standing in the back of the room, trying to keep out of the way. He tried to keep up with what was going on around him, but he couldn't stop thinking about his "gift." Once again, he was able to predict her death by the smell. Even though he hadn't realized it at the time, he was certain that the smell was linked to her death. What he couldn't figure out was whether he had caused her death, the same way he had been partially to blame for Sam. If he hadn't teased Sam and let him win the race, Sam might not have died. And if he hadn't reacted badly to his mother's friend, she might not have fallen and hit her head. *Was she so overcome with my reaction to her bad smell that it killed her? Maybe it gave her a heart attack?* He knew that the smell was linked to death, but he wasn't sure about his role in this whole thing.

Larry's mom pulled on his arm, and he shook his head to snap back to the present. He wondered how to explain what he'd done this time. He looked at her just in time to see a hand coming at his face. She slapped him very hard and pummeled his shoulders with her fists. Larry couldn't imagine what he had done to deserve this treatment.

He knew his mom had a hard life. She worked too many hours for too little pay. She always wanted life to be simple and normal. Most days, he knew, she also wanted a simple, normal child. Certainly, she didn't like the fact that her husband had run out on her and their child. She hadn't heard from Larry's father in years, and she received no support from him or his family. Her one and only social outlet was her friends, the coffee ladies, who got together and talked about other people's issues and problems so their own problems didn't seem as bad as they actually were. She knew her son was one of the hot topics in town, being a little off from the other kids. She also knew that the women had included her in their group mostly so they could get closer to Larry and check him out for themselves. His treatment of her friend this afternoon meant social isolation.

She knew he couldn't help it. She didn't understand the whole "smell" thing, but she could tell that it troubled her son. The slap had been just a release of years of frustration. It wasn't directed at Larry as much as it was at the world in general.

There certainly was no sympathy from the coffee group at the slap. They felt this was a long time coming; she should have done something more with the boy when he was a child and maybe he would not be so weird now.

"It was a long time coming," said one.

"He deserved it," another agreed.

Larry's mom continued to vent her built up anger at life. Everything came pouring out now. "How did you know this? How do you know it? How could you know she was going to die? It's times like this I miss your father. He

was here one day and—*bam*—gone the next.
Maybe he'd know what to do with you now."

In truth, she often found it hard to cope,
being locked into her life with her only son.
Yes, she loved him. But why did she have to
pay so high of a price for love when others
didn't? The love she had squandered on a man,
a man she married, who suddenly left one day
without a note or a goodbye of any kind. The
love of a son, who she hoped would someday be
somewhat normal. But Larry seemed to have
the same bad luck in love as she did and had to
work so hard for it as well.

She felt badly for slapping him in front
of the ladies. She knew that the phone lines
would be hot this afternoon when the women
got home and started spreading the tale of
today's events. She was the only person that
Larry had any kind of love for and the only
person to give Larry love. Now she'd hurt him.
But she would have to deal with his hurt

feelings later. Right now, she needed to cry for her friend. In fact, she just needed to cry in general.

Chapter Five
Realized Gift

After talking about his private moments with his mother, Larry was a bit embarrassed. It was still hard for him to talk about his relationship with his parents, or parent. Both men looked down at the ground and sat quietly on the park bench. The rustling of the leaves was the only sound. Both seemed to have a better understanding of each other and of the events that had twisted their lives together. Larry considered whether he wanted to share any more or leave things as they were. The old man was similarly considering whether to broach a new topic to break the tension. Larry thought about how much time had passed from that time they met. In some ways, it seemed like yesterday; in others, it seemed like the events of his childhood had happened many lifetimes ago. Both where different people now.

He looked warily at the old man. Surprisingly, he didn't react in the way Larry had expected. It was as if the old man had already known.

Larry went on. "I also realized that I could foresee—*fore-smell*—someone's death. I could somehow smell it on them. I could actually tell when someone was going to die. That was my special gift. That was my special talent. To someone else, it would be like getting the answer to the meaning of life. To me, I realized why I was 'weird.'"

The only other talent Larry had developed over time was his answer scripts, his pre-thinking of what he would say.

"I suppose I knew it the day Sam died, the day I met you. The other kids probably knew it too. That's why they stayed away. Like they thought I was *causing* the death. Quite frankly, it scared them too much. They wondered, 'what if one day Larry smelled it on us?' Would they really want to know that they were going to die?

That's when they decided not to hang around with me anymore. That's when the taunting started."

Larry fell silent again.

"That sounds like a weird talent. If you could call it that," the old man said out loud. In fact, it surprised him that he *had* said it aloud. What he said was honest, but blunt. He was afraid that Larry would think he was judging him, taunting him, like his childhood tormenters had. He waited for Larry to respond.

"I know it's an odd talent," Larry said softly. He didn't like the thought of being weird. But he had trained himself to think of his gift as a "talent" over the years. But even he had to admit that it was weird. He thought about other people's talents—Tim's talent to make people laugh, Mike's talent to make any situation more fun, Paul's talent for conversation. They all seemed so normal compared to his. He had wished his gift away a thousand times, wished that he could trade places with any of the other boys just to be normal. Somehow it still seemed so unfair.

Larry chuckled sadly. "Yes. It's definitely an odd talent. I still wonder why only I can smell it. Why only me? Even more, why *me*? Why did my gift have to expose me to the ridicule of others? Why was it everything I did different; why did everything I say come out wrong? Why me?"

The cop sat looking at Larry for a time, waiting to see if Larry would continue with his narrative. After his last misstep, he wanted to think before speaking. He tried to come up with something positive to say. He wanted to say something to make Larry feel better, to make that sad little boy he remembered from the lake feel okay with his life. "I guess if everyone had it, it wouldn't be a gift, now would it?"

"Not really. No."

The old man knew that talking with someone can sometimes be like driving a car. Sometimes, when you hit a dead end, you just want to stop the drive altogether. He didn't want to end the conversation at this dead end. He wanted to keep going so that Larry would not do what he had to do. "Did you ever tell anybody else about it? About smelling death?"

After a moment, Larry replied, "It's easier to show someone your gift for art or singing. How do you show this, and why would you want to?"

He paused and then added, "So much is lost because we don't want to see what others can do, especially when we can't do those things ourselves. Sometimes it's out of jealousy. Sometimes fear. Sometimes confusion. I don't know exactly why. All I know is that people didn't take kindly to my talking about it. I remember people coming over to my house when I was younger. They were friends of the family. I could smell the stink on them. That smell would just hang on them like mothballs on an old coat. It seemed to grow stronger on some of them as time passed. But most people just don't want to know…"

They both sat listening to the wind blow by. They glanced at each other, waiting to see who would speak first. The two just stared at one another, as if the first person to speak would have lost some undefined game. It was a game they had had played so many times before. Uncharacteristically, Larry broke the silence.

"You know, my mom never really believed that I had anything to do with the deaths. Or, maybe she felt she had to believe that I was innocent. I was her son after all. Maybe it was just too much to think that someone she gave birth to and lived in the same house with could have anything to do with death.

"Once, out of the blue, she said to me, 'I know you haven't done anything wrong, no more than someone does wrong by reading a book. You read people's deaths as most read books. Kind of like a sign. I don't know if that's a good thing or a bad thing. I just know I don't want to know about it anymore. And I don't want you to tell me if you know when I'm going to die.'"

The old man was surprised at Larry's revelation. He sat up straight and looked Larry over. Not just at his face, but all over. The old man was seeing him with new eyes. He had a better understanding of Larry now. Often, when you take time to understand someone, to really get to know him, you get a different view of that person based on the life they've lived.

His view of Larry had changed many times over the years. Every time he ran into Larry, his view changed a little bit. Other people must've had similar experiences with him and, possibly, the same thoughts. In the end, even if most people felt sorry for Larry, they also felt terrified of him. He wondered if Larry understood this and couldn't resist asking him.

Even Larry's own mother had been scared of his knowing when she would die. The old man was also terrified, as he was sure that Larry knew the time of his death.

"So, you never told anybody else that you smelled death or maybe—"

"—maybe *caused* death? Is that what you wanted to add?"

That wasn't exactly what the cop was going to say, but, now that Larry had put it out there, he realized that it was a good question to ask. Many people must've asked Larry that. At one time, the old man had also considered it. But now he knew that Larry had been aware of what people had thought.

He simply nodded.

The whole thing was very painful for Larry to talk about. He considered this a "scary" conversation. Just as people were scared of Larry and what he might know, Larry was scared of people and what they might think about him. In truth, Larry was not a cold person. He actually cared for people too much to kill them. He just found it easiest to love them from afar. Some people you can *only* love afar. If you spend time with them, you lose the love and grow to hate them. But to kill someone—no. He did have a heart after all.

He could see that the old man was waiting for an answer to the question. Unfortunately, Larry himself wasn't sure how he should answer it. But he took a deep breath and, again, just let go, skipping the prescribed script. He decided that it was time to say what needed to be said.

"One of the kids at school once told me that he thought I killed Sam that day at the lake," Larry began. "I mean, *really* killed him...rock to the head. None of my friends who were there that day set him straight. The rumor got started, and soon it was the truth. After that, they all just stayed away from me. Sometimes, a person can become a reminder of a lost loved one or a bad moment in his or her life. People like to stay away for that reason alone. Mostly, though, they stayed away because they were scared of me." Larry paused, adding, "Unless you were a cop looking for answers."

Larry chuckled a little and nudged his companion. He was remembering how the old man had hunted him down looking for answers a few years after the incident with the coffee group.

"Why do you say that?" the old man asked, as if he didn't already know. He thought they had both gotten past that. He had harassed Larry. Apparently, it was still a bitter point with the younger man. Apparently, Larry had more that needed to be aired. He was like a house that had been closed up for the winter, patiently waiting for spring to come. Today was that day for Larry, and he was opening up all the windows to let some let some fresh air in and let out some of the ghosts of winter. The old man thought that it was best not to try to stop him from what he needed to say. And, perhaps if Larry opened up, he could help him cope with what had happened.

"So, did you kill them?" The old man asked softly.

Larry looked at him long and hard, then sat back and put out his prepared answer. "I no more killed them than did the man reading the headstone. They were marked for death by someone else. I thought you understood that. So why do you keep asking?"

"I couldn't drop it. Not back then. I thought you were innocent, but then you dropped out of school and disappeared for years. That type of behavior raises suspicion. What happened during that time?"

Larry knew that the question the old man really wanted to ask was "Why did you stop killing people?" And he knew that, even if he explained the truth, the old man still wouldn't believe him.

Larry thought back to those years. He had spent most of his time watching television, since the other kids didn't want anything to do with him. His mom seemed to be okay with that. She knew he didn't have anything better to do. At least it keep him busy and out of trouble. Mostly he would just sit inside watching cop shows. One thing he learned from those shows is that, when a trail goes cold, something has to change to keep the investigation going. People seemed to stop dying around Larry. The trail went cold.

It wasn't cold though. In truth, Larry had merely learned to keep his thoughts to himself. If he smelled death on someone, he'd stay away from the person and keep it to himself. He didn't want to know or draw any attention to himself.

The old man sat patiently waiting for the answer to his question. Where did Larry go, and what happened to him until they met up again years later?

The answer was simple really. Thinking back on it, he had a big event in his life that changed everything. "I got married," he said.

The old man was taken aback. *How did that happen? Who would ever marry Larry? It would have to be a very tolerant woman to marry someone as awkward as him.* Instead, in a tone of voice that was a feeble attempt to hide his still surprised demeanor, he asked, "Did she know about your smelling thing?"

Larry knew that he wasn't asking what he really wanted to know: *did you hide your weirdness or did she just not see it until after you got hitched?* It was going to take some time to explain this one. You can't just jump in the middle of something like that. How do you start? It was more complicated than a simple yes or no.

Chapter Six
Please Don't Let it be Her

Larry was walking down the sidewalk. It had been ten years since he had decided to leave school. The teasing eventually took its toll on him. After a couple of tries, he passed the GED exam and enrolled at a community college the next state over. And he made sure never to mention his "gift." He called his mother for their weekly chat, but he never went back. Larry made damned sure that the freaky little boy he had once been had disappeared completely.

The sun was shining down as Larry strolled along soaking in the brilliant rays. But the pleasure of the afternoon was soon disrupted by his old friend calling on him again. His friend that constantly followed him and reminded him that any truly enjoyable day was merely a dream. Something within a five foot radius was emitting that horrid smell, warning

Larry that whatever it was was close to death. And from the strength of the aroma, it was going to be dead very soon.

Larry awkwardly glanced around in an attempt to figure out where the smell was emanating. Or rather, who the smell was coming from. But should he? Did he really want to know? Sometimes his sense was more of a curse than a gift—did he really want to know who would die soon?

As he looked from person to person, his eyes met those of an older woman walking his way. She smiled at Larry in a sweet simple manner that gave joy to his heart. *Please don't let it be her*, Larry thought to himself. *Not someone so kind and loveable*!

Larry had smelled hundreds of deaths since his granddad's. Some of them affected him more than others. Sometimes, the smell came from a mean, selfish person. Sometimes, it came from an innocent child. Although it was never easy to cope with someone's impending death, his experiences with the kind people stuck in his head longer.

Larry just smiled a sad smile back at the old woman. He knew he couldn't, or rather wouldn't, tell her this unwanted news. In fact, Larry knew that it was best to get away from her as quickly as he could. He had learned from his past that it was best if he wasn't around anymore when someone was about to die. People tended to get suspicious about that sort of thing. Too many questions popped up. It was easier to run away. He also wanted to get away from the smell; it was strong on her, meaning her time was soon.

Larry was stressed, so he quickly pulled out his keychain and started to play with it. He lowered his eyes and, moving away from the older lady to the outside of the sidewalk, he quickly picked up his pace to make his getaway. He was moving so quickly he didn't notice someone else coming down the sidewalk. Larry and the oncoming person collided with a thud, both almost falling to the ground. Larry could easily see he out weighted her, and really almost made her fall. Worst yet, Larry recognized her. It was Pam, his short-fused wife. *Oh crap*, thought Larry. This wasn't a typical thought when you see your spouse, but he had run into her. He had hit the hornet's nest. Larry knew she was really going to make him pay for acting strangely in public again.

Well, this day has gone downhill fast! He prepared for the tongue lashing she was about to give him.

Pam had been out shopping without Larry as she liked to do. Since it was nice outside, she had sent Larry on his way for the day so she could have some down time without him. One thing she wanted to do was to have a smoke. She had told Larry that she had quit before they got married, but she lied and she still smoked. She would find ways to get away. Her "down time," as she called it. Really, it was a smoke break. She promised herself she'd quit, but not today. She had planned to meet him back home later, after shopping. Lucky she had put out her last smoke before running into him. Like most people, she needed time away from Larry. She loved him, but sometimes she just needed a break from him. Sometimes, she needed time to be herself without putting up a front. Time when she didn't need to be so nice. Being around people just took all the niceness out of her. It was one thing she had loved about being single—the "me times." She didn't get much of that anymore.

But being married to Larry had an upside. She now had two incomes to spend, which greatly helped when she went clothes shopping, her favorite hobby. She'd never tell Larry that, though. She couldn't let on that being married to him had some perks. She knew she could get someone better looking who made more money than Larry, but why? He was so easily trained! Some women like men they can break or train like a wild horse. Pam didn't care to spend her time doing that, just too much work. Life was much too short for that. She just simply wanted her way, and Larry let her have her way the majority of the time. His mom had broken him in already for her. That was also another upside for Pam, but he would never know of it.

As this thought was going through her head, bam! Someone ran into her! "Who the devil wasn't paying attention and slammed into me?" she thought, desperately clinging on to her shopping bags as she was spun around. "Who did this? I can't wait to give them a piece of my mind!" Before she could start, she realized the person who she ran into her was her own freaky husband Larry.

"No! It can't be" she thought.

Pam was so ready to unload all her frustrations on someone else. She had gone from store to store and through rack after rack without finding the things she wanted. And top it all off they were out of some of her favorites at the grocery store. She needed to release her annoyance from shopping as well as being bumped. Now, she realized it was Larry who had nearly knocked her over. She would express her frustrations to Larry, but this was not the right time to yell at him. He just didn't get it when he had the weird look on his face. She had to say something though.

"Larry, what are you doing? Walk where you're looking or look where you're walking! I just can't take you out in public anymore, and why the hell are you wearing that shirt? Did I say it was okay to leave the house wearing that? I told you before, I hate that shirt. You need to stop wearing it out of the house or around me. Oh, what am I going to do with you? What are you doing to me?"

Pam absolutely hated how Larry dressed. She thought he looked like a nerd. In truth, Larry really was a bit of a nerd. He did work with computers, she knew, but he didn't have to dress like it.

Out of the corner of her eye, Pam also noticed that the nice old lady Larry was practically running away from had stepped forward to offer sympathy. "Oh, my, are you all right, dear?" she had begun, but she recoiled and scuttled off when Pam started into Larry. This old lady couldn't be a sweeter person, Pam thought, and she started to get angry at herself as well as Larry. She was upset before, but now she was getting really mad; and the more she thought about it, the madder she was getting. She couldn't let this go, and her anger came pouring out.

Using her most stern voice, she told Larry, "I'll never understand why you freak out over some people. You almost trip over yourself getting out of their way! I've seen you get sick to your stomach at the sight of someone you don't even know. You almost run away from them, trying to get away. It could be someone you have known for years, and then one day act like they have some bad cologne on. And, I'm still really pissed at you for the day you were so rude to my friend Jen and freaked out over her. You wouldn't even be in the same room as her! The next day she died! Now you can never tell her you're sorry for being a jerk and acting so weird around her, making her feel bad about herself."

Larry, being as well trained as he was, knew he was going to pay heavily for running into Pam. And whatever he said would only make her angrier with him. Larry therefore thought it best to keep to himself and not say anything. He knew he was lucky to have her as his wife. He better not make too big of a deal out of anything and just say he was sorry, which he did.

Larry wondered what Pam was doing there. Then he wondered what he was doing there.

He looked around. They were standing in front of the stairs that led up to their apartment. He had absent-mindedly walked back home. He had been so busy enjoying the air that he meandered back home without realizing it.

Their apartment was on top of one of the stores that lined the street. At one time, it had been the main street of the town. Then a strip mall popped up outside of town, causing the shopping to move to that area. Now most of the shops on Main Street were antique shops with apartments above them. He liked it there. There was a park around the corner with a lake. It was a nice place to live—a smaller town, but close to a major city. Most people worked in the larger city but lived here, a town that had kind of lost its soul and now was a place to sleep at night.

Some called this kind of town a bedroom town, because you spent most of your waking hours in the big city, only returning home to sleep.

Pam began pulling at Larry's arm, leading him like a puppy upstairs to their apartment. She could see in his eyes that he was off again, someplace in his mind day dreaming, thinking about something that had nothing to do with her. It was time to reel him back in to her world. He seemed to have that look on his face from time to time, as if no one was home.

He said nothing after she snapped him back from his thoughts and walked behind her. He was waiting to see if she had cooled down before talking. He really hoped she had. He walked in the apartment after her. The apartment windows were open, letting in the fresh air and sounds of the street below in the apartment. Through the open windows, Larry could see the people going up and down the sidewalks, enjoying the nice Saturday of cool fall weather. He could see much of the sleepy town from the front room as he looked down on the spot where he had bumped into Pam. He was still a little stressed from Pam's being mad at him, and he pulled out his keychain and started to rub it between his fingers to claim himself down.

While Pam was making noise putting away some food items she had bought, he could hear sirens getting louder from the windows. They seemed to be coming closer and closer to Main Street. He looked around, trying to see signs of why they were approaching. He should have known.

He spotted the old lady he had smelled death on sitting on a bench outside one of the stores across the street. She was surrounded by people attempting to help her. At first glance, it seemed that she might have a heart attack. Pam broke Larry's thought by filling the air with her words.

"Sounds like the meat wagon is coming to get someone again. Someone else kicked the bucket." Pam could be rather crass and cold-hearted at times, or rather most of the time.

"That's a pretty crude way to put it," Larry responded. Then he remembered she was mad at him, and he should keep his mouth shut. She had just yelled at him for being cold and rude, for running into her. However, Pam was being just as cold.

Pam was still busy putting away groceries when she noticed Larry was off in never-never land again in one of his day dreams. He should be feeling bad for running away from the old lady, so she decided to snap him out of it. She wanted to start in on the guilt trip she had planned for him. There was no cancelling that trip, unlike their last vacation! Larry had made the mistake of adding a comment when she was still angry with him, and now it was time for her to close the door on any more comments he might want to make and call him out on his last one.

"Me? What about you calling it someone's 'expiration date'? You say I'm cold?"

She thought, "That should keep him in check for now… ."

Larry knew it was really time for him to keep his mouth closed. He was, after all, well trained. Back down on the street, he watched the play being acted out in front of him. It was one he'd seen way too many times in his life—Sam, his granddad, and eventually his mother. Most of all, he already knew the ending of the final act. The old lady appeared to be coming around. She looked at the people standing next to her, then up, and she noticed Larry standing in the window looking down at her. Watching it all happen, he looked like a nicer person than when she first saw him on the street. But now he had a different look to him, one not of this world. She knew who—or what—he was; it was clear. She raised her left hand slowly and weakly toward Larry and called out.

"No! Not yet!"

She seemed to be speaking to Larry. But he was not near her, nor could he help her anyway. The fact that she addressed him shocked Larry. It was as if she knew he could smell death on her and believed that, somehow, he knew how to stop it. As the old lady spoke, those around her also looked up to see where she seemed to be pointing and directing her words. Everyone looked at Larry. He just stood quietly in shock.

Chapter Seven
Last Eye Contact

It was a slow day for the town cop as he turned onto sleepy Main Street. He, along with many other local citizens, was enjoying the Saturday's nice, cool, fall weather. He was walking partly to enjoy the weather and partly to make his doctor happy. His doctor had been complaining about how he had put on some extra weight and needed to exercise more. So he decided to do it at work; indeed of driving the car, walked the streets on his rounds. He was at the top of the street when he received a call regarding an older lady having some health problems on Main. She wasn't far from where he was, so he picked up the pace a bit and began a light jog to the area in question. As he came closer, he could see a small group of people surrounding someone sitting on a bench. He began to disperse the crowd so he could help her.

A little winded, he asked the crowd in a loud authoritative voice, "I know you all want to help, but, for the love of Pete, give the lady some air!"

He observed that the woman was talking. Her voice was weak and not very easy to understand. She was holding her left arm up in the air pointing.

As he followed the angle of her arm upward, he saw Larry. The cop had a sudden epiphany, "That was the kid from the lake and the teenager from when the chubby lady bit the dust during coffee! And I bet he's playing with that keychain he was always carrying." He had not seen him for some time, almost forgotten about him. But here was someone dying, and here was Larry again. Yeah, he might have caught glimpses of Larry around town, but not like this, eye-to-eye again. As he squinted to get a better view, he clearly saw that is *was* the same person. And, as he had suspected, Larry was playing with something in his hand, but the cop couldn't make out what it was from such a distance.

The officer was aware that murders sometimes took "trophies," from their victims—personal items that the killer could use to remember his crime. He wondered if that was why the keychain was so significant to Larry. Suspicions arose again. For the moment, though, he turned away from Larry and back to the lady on the bench, still moaning in pain. He filed Larry's location away for further questioning though.

After making eye contact with the old lady and seeing her pointing at him, Larry stepped back from the window to get out of sight of the people on the street. But not fast enough. He had not let himself be around someone he smelled dying for some time now for just this reason. Now he was spotted around another death, by that cop, of all people. Larry had used his power of smelling death to stay clear of those who were dying. Now he had failed in his goal of being inconspicuous. He thought again, "This lovely day has gone downhill, and much worse, incredibly fast!"

Even though Larry took a step back, he could still see what was going on down on the street. He mainly didn't want the cop to see him. Larry watched the play unfold in front of him, waiting for the last act. He knew it would come soon. It was good she was dying in the fall, if she had to die. He noticed that some people die in the spring. If he could pick his end, it would be in the fall, just as winter started. He would hate to live though the cold of winter only to die and miss out on spring and the beginning of summer.

Before this thought could really drift by, he noticed something new. *This is weird*, he thought. He hadn't seen this before. Someone changed the script of the play! A new act had been added. He saw a large flash of light by the lady and what seemed to be a man all dressed in black. It was just for a second. It was so fast his eyes struggled to see it. But he did see it; he saw what it was. It was just long enough for him to see and for his brain to pick it up. He had witnessed something new.

"What was that all about?" he wondered out loud.

"What are you talking about, Larry?" Pam demanded from the other room.

Pam didn't know much about Larry's ability to smell death on others, and Larry didn't care to tell her. If he did, it would be just one more thing she could use as a tool when she was upset at him. He found it best not to tell her too much; it just armed her with things to use on one of her harangues against him.

"Well?" Pam added impatiently.

Maybe if he just didn't say anything, she would go on with putting the groceries away and forget all about it. He loved her, but one of the things he liked best about being with her was that he could just get lost in his own world and she would—usually—leave him alone. She would be so into her own world that she tended to forget he was even there in the same apartment with her. Larry really liked that. He glanced over in Pam's direction, hoping she had moved on to something else. He wanted to see if she had registered his comment. Unfortunately for Larry, she had, and she was now impatiently waiting for more information about his interest in the activity across the street.

Pam had put away most of the items in the kitchen and now had time to talk with Larry, or work on him, whichever way you looked at it. However, she had changed her mind about chewing him out this time. She had other plans for him. Sometimes, she liked to make it known to Larry that she cared for him. She would write down and keep track of the times she talked to him politely, that way, she didn't overdo it, nor would Larry get used to it and then require it all the time. She believed that too much of a good thing could get him used to it. Then he wouldn't appreciate it when she did make an effort. Yes, quality time had to be rationed. And it was best to keep that amount of time on the low side. She felt the same way about sex. If they were to have sex every day, then it wasn't special. Pam was all about making conversation and sex seem special to Larry. She wanted him constantly to hungry for both.

However, she did break the rule occasionally and spend more time talking to him than usual. Today was going to be one of those times. While Larry would usually have appreciated her interest, today was *not* one of those times. Larry's fascination with the old lady and officer across the street piqued her interest. She wanted to know more about his strange behavior earlier, and his strange behavior now. She was determined to find out more. And she made sure that she always got her way.

Pam started off in a soft tone talking to him, in a baby-like voice. "So, what's weird, Mr. Weirdo—I mean, Larry?"

Pam thought it always helped to insult him a little. She felt that it seemed to get him going in a conversation easier, put him on the defense to prove he was not a weirdo. He had to justify his behavior. And Pam was very interested in his current behavior.

Larry hated how Pam always seemed to cut him down. He felt that he had to prove himself over and over again. In his eyes, it was just a pain in the backside. Why couldn't she just be nice instead of badgering him? He hated it and hated when she quizzed him. Every time she did, it just shut him down and made him close up and not talk with her. This was better for Larry. And today, more than any other, Larry decided he was going to do what he always did when she acted like that. He just simply closed down, pulled back, let his eyes glaze over, and went someplace else in his mind.

He shrugged and softly told her, "Nothing. Just something I saw on the street. You had to be there."

As Larry said this, he walked away from her and sat down at the kitchen table. He thought his statement would divert her and get her to some new topic, but it didn't work this time. She followed him and began asking more questions.

"What's with you? You know I love you, but this weirding-out stuff has to go. You act like this over people on the street? And even now, I can tell there is more to it than you're telling me. I know it has to do with something you smelt. But you will never tell me what's going on with you and this smell thing. What's wrong with you? Why don't you trust me to tell me? Don't you love me?"

Larry felt Pam was clueless sometimes even more then she pretended to be. She had the hardest time picking up the hints he left her. Larry decided to try one more time to let her know that he really didn't want to talk about it. It was a typical, boring Larry hint. He just shrugged his shoulders and said nothing. He turned back to the windows that faced the street.

Pam was now getting extremely mad at Larry. She wanted her way, and Larry was breaking that rule. She was going to work him over and find out somehow. It seemed to give her joy when she got her way, maybe because she liked to win. She decided she was going to hit him hard with the questions. She had reason to. She had information for him, but she needed him to fill in some of the blanks first before she could tell him. She decided before she would tell him her news, he'd have to answer her questions to her liking. Her news was very big. The information she had was the biggest thing that she had ever told him and possibly the biggest news she would ever tell him in their lives together. It was even bigger than the day she told him she would marry him. But right now, Larry needed to tell her what she wanted to know. She decided to try one of her old tricks that seemed to work with him in the past.

She said, "I married you even though all my friends and family told me you were a nice man but a little off. With that said, don't you think I'm entitled to more? I do a lot for you. Why won't you tell me? Or at least stop doing your weird freaky sideshows? Pick one, any one of them, but just pick one. I would love you more if you just told me. Better yet, tell me and stop the freak act. *That* would really show you love me."

As Pam talked, she tossed her hands up in the air making all kinds of dramatic movements. She believed this helped sell the point and eventually he'd open up to her. In truth, it drove Larry crazy. If he died and went to hell, he was sure that the devil would torment him with an endless barrage of gesticulating women. He believed it made her look like a monkey during mating season. She was now even more upset that he hadn't answered her yet. However, she did enjoy forcefully extracting information out of him. It made it a challenge, one she always won. It made her feel powerful. She waited impatiently for Larry to answer.

Larry, at this point, figured that she wasn't going to give up on her inquisition. He decided to fight fire with fire. "Freak sideshows?" Immediately after saying that, he copied her wild hand movements and added some armpit scratching to the dance. He could see it upset her.

"No! You did not just do that!" yelled a very angry Pam.

Larry knew he was in deep trouble now. He had hoped his recreation of her arm movements would distract her, but it didn't work. Pam put her hands on her hips, tilted her head to the left side, and glared at him for about a full minute. Without moving, she shouted, "It's like you just smelled a bad fart or smelled Hell itself! Then you choked and freaked out! People just stop and stare at you. Can't you see how badly that looks?"

Pam's face had a nice solid cherry red tone to it at this point. Larry could tell that Pam had a renewed passion for finding out why he moved away from some people. She didn't know he could smell death, and he would hate to tell her what he was *really* smelling. It was common for her to keep on him about it, but today she was really going all out. She had her guns loaded and ready to fire. Larry was hoping she would not do the whole hand waving in the air thing again. The one good thing about her hand thing was it made the fun parts of her body jump up and down, which kind of turned him on. But when you go so long without sex, the crack of day turns you on. It was definitely the parts he liked to see bounce that way on his wife. He would never dare tell her that though. She would have gone out of her way to stop have her chest move, holding them down somehow, many even putting on a sports bra before she yelled at him. Something more important was said this time that lingered in his thoughts.

He thought about what she had said about smelling Hell. What does Hell smell like? Was Pam right? Was he actually smelling Hell on these people?

He returned his attention to Pam. "Hell? So what do you think Hell smells like?"

Pam was getting angrier and angrier. She did enjoy extracting information from Larry, but that was wearing off now. She needed to find out what was going on with him, and she wanted to know right now! The information she was going to share with Larry really needed to be said. It was, after all, life changing information for both of them. Pam decided to use another trick she'd used on Larry in the past and worked. She was a little surprised he tried to get her off the topic, and now she was going to let him know she was on to him. She would win the game.

"I don't know! How the hell would I know? Read the Bible, or a book, or something! We are not getting into what I might think Hell smells like, damn it! Why are you so weird about this? Why won't you talk to me about it?" It was time to go in for the kill. "I thought we told each other everything! I tell *you* everything. Like last week, for example, when Jane thought she was pregnant? I told you, didn't I?"

"What?" Larry asked. "What the hell does Jane's pregnancy scare have to do with anything?"

Pam was really mad, and it was very obvious for Larry to see. "Now you're just trying to piss me off! You know that makes me mad! I hate that. Why do you freak out like that sometimes? Don't you love me?" Pam was starting to cry, and Pam was not a person who cried much. When she did, it was mostly to get her way. She let the tears fall where they may, and watched to see how Larry would react.

Larry felt like a wild animal locked in a cage. He just wanted out! Pam knew she had to go for one more try before Larry made up some reason why he had to leave and ran to the door.

In a soft, caring, hurt, tone of voice said, "Larry, I work hard. I don't ask for much. We live in this hell-hole of an apartment. It's not a nice house like my friends have. I still wear the clothes I bought before we got married so we can save up for a house someday. I put my faith and trust in you. We don't have much. We don't have a lot of friends because of your weirdness. But, maybe, you can put your faith and trust in me and tell me? That's all I ask."

She could see by his face that she'd touched some of Larry's emotions. He actually was thinking about telling her. Could he? Pam, seeing Larry conflicted, needed one final push. She knew she was close to getting what she wanted.

Larry just stood there. He was dumbfounded. She might have pushed him a little too hard. He realized it was time to back it down a little. Before Larry could really say anything, Pam added, "The only thing that could make me happy right now is for you to tell me why you do that weird crap around people. It freaks out my friends and family. Hell, it freaks out anybody who sees it. Not to mention, your co-workers! No wonder you never get ahead in your job and we're stuck in this dump!"

One of Larry's most watched movies was *Who's Afraid of Virginia Woolf*. He loved the line, "What a dump!" Pam hated when he used that line. However, she found herself using the word "dump" a lot. It gave her the chance to use it before he could. Pam could see he was getting ready to use the phrase as they did in the movie. She wasn't going to allow that! She interrupted by saying, "And don't do the movie line 'What a dump!' from that movie you like so much." Pam turned her head sideways, looked angrily at him, to let him know that she was just short of losing it. She realized, though, that she had pushed too far. Larry walked past her, not saying a word, and went into the bedroom and plopped himself on the bed. Pam let him go, realizing her interrogation needed a break. And all this hard work on Larry had made her hungry. She decided to start dinner instead.

Larry had been beaten up verbally by Pam before, but not like this. This time, she had set an all-time record. *Time to call the book of world records*, he thought. She hit him hard this time. It was times like this when he wondered why the two of them stayed married. Usually, Pam's interrogations didn't bother him. But today, her actions had hit a nerve. He just wanted the interrogation to stop. If he wanted this kind of beating, he would have worked overtime with his boss.

His head was spinning. He wasn't ready to break down and tell her yet. He needed to think about it and plan exactly how he was going to tell her. Larry needed time away from her. He was scared of what she might do, if and when he told her. And maybe he would have told her if she had stopped pushing him so much.

He decided that avoidance was the best solution to the fight. As he was lying there, he occasionally dozed off. From time to time, he could hear Pam making extra noise in the kitchen as she cooked dinner, trying to make sure he did not go to sleep. Larry just rolled over and went back to sleep. She never came in once to ask if she was making too much noise with the pots and pans. Once, when the clanging and clanking woke him up, he chuckled to himself. She was trying very hard to get him back into her game, and he just wouldn't play anymore.

She did come in to tell him dinner was ready. Larry didn't want to eat. Even food wouldn't get him up and out of bed today. He needed to rest and let his mind have some down time, time to think about what he wanted to do and how he wanted to do it. He needed to let his mind come up with a solution as his body rested. That seemed to work in the past, and he was determined to let it work again now.

Chapter Eight
Surprisingly Quickly

Larry slowly woke up, realizing it was now morning. He had made it through the night. In his head, he started to sing part of the *Star Spangled Banner*: "Gave proof through the night, that our flag was still there." He had made it. Sometimes it was best not to play.

Larry knew he was still in trouble with Pam. She was going to royally kick his butt now. He had won the battle, but not the war. He could feel her in bed behind him. Their bedroom was small, and the noise of her breathing easy heard off the walls. She was going to give him pure hell because she hadn't gotten her way yesterday. He lay in bed, not moving. If he could keep her from waking up early, she would have to rush into the shower and then run off to work. She wouldn't have any time at all to hit him with more questions or play her silly games. That was his plan, anyway. Aside from that, he didn't like what she had planned for him that night after work.

It's not like he really cared about being cut off from sex, but it seemed so long ago, at least a month or two. Sometimes he thought Pam had joined a convent and just forgot to tell him about it.

Pam rolled over in the bed. She was thinking back on how she had eaten dinner by herself the night before, because she was unable to get Larry up from his nap. He shouldn't do that if he ever wanted to be with her again. She liked keeping him hungry in that department, wanting more so he did not stray. She wanted to simply sit up and watch TV with him. She didn't plan on hitting him with more questions now: Larry wouldn't get up for that either. So, she ate by herself, watched TV by herself, read a book, and went to bed next to him. He wouldn't know anything she'd done that night; it was as if she had a second life without him.

Pam looked at the clock on the night stand. It was getting late, and both she and Larry needed to be at work very soon. As she tried to decide whether to roll back over for another five minutes of sleep, her anger from the night before came flowing back in. *I can't believe he slept all night*, she thought. Then, aloud, "Larry you need to get up for work. You missed dinner, and you missed being with your wife. You missed a lot, but you can't miss work. I won't let you."

Larry didn't seem to care what Pam said. He just rolled away from her, pretending he was still asleep. Annoyed, Pam growled, "Get up. You might not trust me with your 'secret,' but you can trust me to get your ass out of this bed!"

Pam put her feet on Larry's back and pushed him out onto the floor. He fell between the wall and the bed, out of sight.

Without a word, he got up, walked into the bathroom, undressed, and stepped into the shower.

He acted like one of the walking dead, only moving when he had to. "I'll find out your secret one way or another, even if it kills one of us!" she thought. As Larry walked out of the room, Pam reminded him, "Don't forget tonight! I want to see the hypnotist. He helped my friend Darcy and her husband. Who the hell knows? He might pull off some miracle and help you! Don't forget to head over to his place after work. I'll email you the address and meet you in front of his house. Don't be late! And..."

Larry did not show much sign of life. He was only going to do what he absolutely needed to. Pam hurt him a little when she pushed him out of bed. A hot shower would feel good on his sore back. He interrupted Pam on purpose. He already knew the rest of the statement. Larry finished her statement for her by saying, "I know…you can't make me be on time, but if I'm late I'll wish you did." He paused a second and looked at Pam. Pam nodded in agreement and said, "That's right baby."

Larry hated being forced to consult such people. He had spent way too much time with them in the past, like when his mom decided to find out why he was so weird and asked all sorts of wild questions. They would wait for you to say the wrong thing, and go down that path. Each answer only led to more questions. It was their business model that enticed you to keep coming back. Oftentimes, you'd go in with one problem and come out with five new problems.

Larry thought about the last time he and Pam talked about his thing. How he had hated that conversation! Maybe that was why she was bringing this up again? Larry remembered when he she signed him up for this and how he told her about having five new problems at the end of the meeting. She just responded, "You'll be lucky if you only have five!" She always had a way of making something painful seem even more painful than he had expected. She could kick it up and make it over the top—that was her gift. Just when he thought things couldn't get worse, Pam would put it in new light, making it even bigger and more painful.

This time, Larry kept his mouth shut. He had learned. And besides, it was time to go to work. Unfortunately for Larry, his boss could be Pam's brother with the similar games they both played. He was not sure why he had so many of these types in his life. It was as if he somehow called out to them and they came running his way. He like his boss that had hired him, but that boss quit after he had been there only a month. A month was all he needed to see the place was messed up, and he went running for the door. Before he had left, he told Larry, "I'm quitting. If you want me to tell you why, I will. You won't like it. But I feel you have a right to know."

Larry decided not to ask. Pam had been on his back about needing a steady paycheck, so he didn't want to incite her wrath by leaving his new job. He knew he would probably learn in time. But he decided to stay blissfully unaware of the company's flaws until he had to. Working in IT, he got to see all of the company's dirty underwear—who got paid what, who got what raise, who got some toy for their home office on the company dime. All that stuff ran by the eyes of the computer department. He knew who his new boss was calling. He had seen the cell phone bills and late night phone calls to the woman in accounting.

Larry got to work. He knew he was late. If only time went as quickly during the day as it did on his way to work. When he walked into the office, everyone was working surprisingly quietly in their 5 by 5 office blocks. The office was set up in rows of cubicles, all in a straight line. The dividers were all the same odd gray tone and low enough to hide if you crouched down, or were sitting. The partitions were supposed to keep you from walking around and talking to others. His boss could see anyone who was standing, walking, talking, or otherwise wasting time.

His jerk of a boss believed that if an employee was happy, the work load was too light. Happily joking workers met too much time on their hands. If he noticed anyone happy, he would give him more work to do. Larry found it funny that most of the studies he'd read recommended just the opposite: a happy worker can, and will, do more than an unhappy worker. Happy workers feel empowered to take on extra work. This thought had not been part of his boss's management style. Then again, calling his management style a "style" would insult the word style. He was sure his boss was the person Jimmy Buffett sang about in the song, *Were You Born an Asshole?*

Larry had the song on his playlist and loved to listen to it at work on his headset. It made him smile to hear it playing and see his boss walking by. It was one of the small joys in life his wife and boss could not take away from him. Somehow, down deep, he was still somewhat alive.

His boss was quite a piece of work, to put it bluntly. He had a foreign accent, but refused to say what country he was from. So no one really knew. He bragged about being two people, one good and one bad. His employees never knew which side would show up that day. Actually, Larry knew that he really didn't have a good side—just "kind of an asshole" and "full on asshole."

His last lie was that he was born in Texas and spent three years in the army with a special troop involved in exploring the culture of other countries. The thought behind the special troop was that by living with the natives and learning to speak their language, they could better infiltrate the enemy. If we ever went to war with that country, they could beat them from within their own walls. He lived for ten years like that. As a result, he no longer knew his own nationality. Nobody could ever tell if Larry's boss was telling the truth or not.

Larry's boss's boss was also a jerk. However, he knew he needed to hire bigger jerks than himself to make himself look less like a jerk. That's how Larry's boss was brought on board. Larry liked to call them "The Jerk Club." Larry called his boss "Jerk Face," and called his boss's boss "King Jerk Face." It was easy to pick them out because the company paid for special company logo shirts for that level, and only them. Nobody at Larry's level or below ever got anything. It was funny how that worked out. They unknowingly made themselves stand out from the others. In their warped minds, it was good for them.

It was a weird office and very noisy at times. Larry tried to work efficiently, but his coworkers were in the habit of raising their voices, to ensure the boss heard them. Yes, they always talk as if the world was coming down and life was going to end over every little thing. It was a show for the boss on how unhappy they were, making sure not to get more work. At times, the noise level would become unbearable for Larry. The racket made it difficult for Larry to work; he would have to do other things to distract himself. Sometimes he'd pretend he was reading email. That way, he at least looked busy while waiting for the noise to abate. Once that happened, he could get some work done.

Each bad day at work, Larry would take out a pen and one piece of paper and write in detail how he really felt about his boss. Then he would take the paper, fold it in half, and put it in the paper shredder box. This was a locked box. Every week, an outside company would pick it up, unlock it, and shred the contents. The box was for all paperwork that had key information on it; this kind of paperwork was not to be tossed in the trash, but in the bin. Larry really wanted to drop it off at his boss's desk, but the box would have to do. Doing that made him feel better. But today, he was already late and sure to get yelled at. He would need to write two letters today.

Arriving at his office, Larry entered by the back door. He tried to get to his desk without anybody noticing; he tried walking in a crouched position to avoid being caught by Jerk Face. No point in looking like he was *trying* to hide. As he headed for his desk, he met Aaron, a co-worker he liked to have lunch with, and talk to. Aaron was one of those people you like at work, but probably wouldn't meet socially. What brought them together was their hatred of their work atmosphere and their hatred of the boss. If one should leave the firm, that would be lost, and the friendship would end.

Aaron was a computer programmer, as was Larry. They worked next to each other in the cubicle firing line. Sometimes, to get away from the noise, they would move into a conference room in order to get some work done. They'd set up a fake meeting, book the room, take their laptop computers in there, and close the door. Larry and Aaron found it funny that the only person who had a door and an office on their floor was their boss, Jerk Face. He didn't need it. He only closed the door when he had a pretty female visitor, or when he was yelling at his wife on the phone.

Aaron met Larry halfway down the hall. Larry could see he had something to tell him. Aaron and Larry watched out for each other. Aaron said, "Good morning man! You're late for work again, but don't let Jerk Face see you. He is really in a bad mood today."

Larry was thankful for Aaron's help, but he wished Aaron had waited until he reached his desk before telling him the news, giving him more of an open lane to his desk.

Larry replied, "Thanks, overslept again. I'm not in the mood to be here, but I really don't want to be at home either. Pam has one of her things planned for tonight, and I'm really not interested. Some days I just want out of this life."

That was true. He wished he could get a new life with a real job where people let him do his work and didn't mess with him. Other employees tended to single out the two because they were computer programmers; other employees didn't understand what they actually did for the company.

Aaron knew that Larry got the short end of the stick with their boss. Aaron got his share, but Larry took a lot more than anyone else in the office. Jerk Face seemed convinced that Larry's spirit hadn't been broken yet. Jerk Face was clueless about computer programming. He had an accounting background and was, technically, an accountant by trade. Computer programmers were in the Information Technology Department. Larry and Aaron never understood why the company always put accounting managers in charge of the Information Technology Department. Because Jerk Face knew little about what Larry and Aaron did for the company, they were constantly harassed and ridiculed by Jerk Face. When Jerk Face would abuse Aaron, he'd just be quiet and take the beating. He wouldn't try to stick up for himself. It worked for him, and he advised Larry to adopt his method. Larry didn't get it, though, and Aaron figured he never would. So, for now, Aaron would just tell Larry "Good luck with that! We all need a new life. By the way, here he comes!"

Frank, also commonly known as Jerk Face, was hot on Larry's trail. He'd seen him come in late again and meant to let him know he'd been caught. Frank was going to make a good example out of him in front of everyone today. Frank considered berating others as an unwritten benefit of his title. Besides, he enjoyed picking on Larry. Larry seemed to have a sign on his back that said "pick on me." So Frank did.

The company was doing great and Frank was getting all kinds of bonuses. He'd never tell his employees that, though, because he and his boss told everyone the company was doing poorly so they wouldn't have to pay bonuses to the employees. The Jerk Club thought that made the employees work harder. But unbeknownst to them, the computer staff wrote the reports and knew that profits were up. They also knew that Frank and his boss were getting big bonuses.

With his oddly broken English, Frank said, "Larry! There you are! I told you that, if you're not at your desk promptly at eight, you need to email the while team and tell us where you were. This is not acceptable! You need to decide whether you still want to work here or not. Do you want me to cut your pay? I'll call HR right now and change your title and pay. I can do that!"

Larry started to sing the Jimmy Buffett song. This was another play Larry had seen before. And, just like his fights with Pam, he already knew how it ended. However, it still stressed him out every time it happened. Larry pulled out his keychain with the birthstone on it and starting playing with it, hoping to calm his nerves. He didn't have to think about it; it was instinctual. Larry had worked late the weekend before and felt inclined to remind Frank. "I put in 20 extra hours last weekend! So if I'm five minutes late it shouldn't be a big deal."

Frank merely replied, "We don't have comp time. You're salaried. You're expected to work overtime and be at your desk 8 to 5 and email the whole team if you're not." As this conversation occurred, Frank and Larry slowly walked toward Larry's cubicle and stopped at Larry's desk. Larry was trying to get away from Frank, but now he was stuck between him and the back wall of his cubicle. Jerk Face was staring him down. He didn't blink, breathe, or move. As he stood looking at Jerk Face, he noticed something that he hadn't noticed before. Today, Frank had that smell on him. Larry tried to look away to avoid the smell. It was painful for Larry to stand next to him. He'd never been this close to Frank, and never wanted to be again. Larry wondered if he'd always had the smell and he'd not noticed it until now.

He just wanted to get away from Frank, but, by the look on the boss's face, he knew something was up. Jerk Face said, in a condescending tone, "Now what's wrong? Did you get the reports done? You were supposed to document everything you do every day and plan what you need to do for the next two weeks in the future. Where are the reports I asked for?"

Larry could smell death on him. It was painful for him to answer, but he did. "Yes. I sent them to you two days ago—the due date."

Larry knew it was just busy work. Jerk Face wouldn't recognize a programming task if it bit him in the butt, so to retaliate. He'd give Larry and Aaron reports to write. He would grade them on these reports, like a teacher grades a student, *without even reading them.* The reports were essentially meaningless, just punishment. This was confirmed when the boss said, rather defensively, "I haven't had time to look at them. I'm busy. Very busy!"

Jerk Face was busy, all right—busy messing with his employees or kissing the back side of King Jerk Face. If Frank was away, he and Aaron could do twice the work in half the time. He made sure he touched Larry's work and messed it up, took some good work and added junk to it, making it junk. He didn't care about what the users wanted, only what he wanted. He had to change things just to change them, to put his messed-up touch on them. Frank was the king of taking someone's great idea and making it a bad project. In one case, a user asked for the total sales for the month. By the time Jerk Face got done with it, it was called "total un-sold items by month" and listed items that didn't sell. When the user asked about what did sell, Jerk Face told the user, "just subtract the not sold items from the inventory at the beginning of the month, and you will get items sold." The user walked away, tossing the report in the trash.

Larry noticed his boss's veins in his face were protruding; still, Larry felt compelled to stick up for himself today. "Yes, we're all busy. By the way, what about the new server project we discussed?"

Frank had put this project off, no doubt to avoid spending money on it. At the end of the year, he always got a bonus for being frugal with the department's money. And Frank had big plans for that money, this year. The IT department needed the new equipment, but Jerk Face wanted to deprive them, keeping them hungry for more. He made sure *he* wasn't deprived.

Out of the corner of his eye, Frank saw his own boss walk by. He felt it was time to kiss some butt. Larry could wait for another day. He told Larry he needed more reports, and they had to be finished before he'd consider purchasing the new server. That tactic always seemed to work for him. Whenever Larry was close to finishing one batch of reports, Frank would assign another wave of work, always providing heavy critique of the previous work. He liked to blame the delay on Larry. In truth, it didn't matter to him if he ever purchased the server. He didn't care as long as he got his bonus. His quickly went through his money—and so did his girlfriend. His bonuses were what kept them happy.

Frank quickly changed his tone of voice and began to smile. Larry was actually thankful to see King Jerk Face walk by; it changed his whole demeanor. It was like he was a totally different person. The veins in Frank's neck were no longer popping out.

Frank took a deep breath and ran down the hall after his boss. "Thank God!" thought Larry. He heard Frank tell his boss, "Mr. Smith, Mr. Smith! How are you today? I was just welcoming our happy workers to work and helping them with a problem they've had with programming. They look up to me, you know."

What a lie, Larry thought. How can someone change so quickly? You have to be bipolar, because Larry was just Larry and he didn't understand some that put up such a fake front. There was a running joke in the office. It went, "How do you know Frank is lying? His lips are moving!"

Aaron was crouched in his cubicle listening to Frank verbally abuse Larry and waited until Frank was on the other side of the office before standing up and making eye contact with Larry, letting Larry know he felt for him. Being in the same battle or work, whatever you wanted to call it, together you sometimes don't need to speak words to understand what the other person is thinking. This was one of those times. Just his look told Larry, "sorry dude." Aaron and Larry could still see Frank walking down the row and knew Frank could see them standing looking his way, if he turned around. At this point, Frank didn't care; Larry and Aaron knew that. Frank only cared about what could make him more money, and he had that in his sights—his boss.

Aaron wanted to say something to Larry to make him feel better. Instead, all he could think of was "Wow! He's hitting you hard, man! He is such an ass to us, but such a kiss ass to his boss! What an asshole."

Larry was thankful that someone understood. "Yeah, he does what he knows: kiss ass and cut costs. He knows nothing about the computer systems we use or what we do." Aaron knew this was true. Typically, companies have the Information Technology Department report to someone that had an accounting background, but they only see the computer staff as a number on a spreadsheet.

Every year, the accounts would look at that spreadsheet to see who they could get rid of, how they can lower salaries and increase their personal bonus. Frank had not made it as an accountant for just this reason. In his last job with a different company, he believed the Sales Department should bring in the money, and his job was to not spend it. So, when the Sales Department would ask for purchases, he'd deny them. That didn't work very well, and sales started to decline as a result. Frank got fired. But he still didn't realize why he had been let go of; he believed that the company just wanted to relocate the job to the corporate office. He was clueless about what people thought of him, as if his own big head somehow blocked out the reality of how people hated him. Larry knew Frank's goal was not to spend money on computers and other technical equipment, forcing the employees to keep the old equipment working.

Larry knew what Aaron was thinking. They were all just expenses to Frank. Not workers, not people, just costs. However, Larry knew from the strong odor that Frank would die soon.

"Thank God he's going to die soon." *Crap! Did I just say that out loud*? He had, and now he'd get all kinds of questions from Aaron.

And, of course, he did. "What did you say? How do you know Joe will be dead soon? What the hell man? You aren't going to do something stupid, are you?"

Larry wondered how he was going to get himself out of this. He told Aaron something he had learned in his last job. "I meant to say, he'll be leaving the company soon. Sorry man. I didn't mean to say it that way. Only if he goes, we might end up with someone even more of a pain and clueless. I've seen it before." Larry hoped that would distract Sam enough to get off the topic for now.

Their coworker, Esther, overheard their conversation from the cubicle next to them. She had worked at the company for about two years. She liked it there. She was also a programmer but was terrible at it. She had a good position at this company. It was one of the few places she could work and not really do anything. She spent most of her day working on office politics. If someone questioned her programming skills, she would try to destroy them socially and ruin their work reputation. Her strongest talent was tattling on people. She had dirt on everyone. That was, essentially, her job, to gather gossip and information about others so she could use it against them later. If Frank came her way looking to get on her about something, she'd interrupt him and tattle on someone. Frank didn't always want to hear her information, but, now that it was out there, he would lose his original train of thought and focus on what Esther just told him. Then, Frank turn his attention away from her to go after the person Esther had mentioned. That always made her smile. She had a wicked smile, but didn't overuse it. Her smile could frighten children. She was missing several teeth, and the remaining teeth were rotting in her mouth. Esther smoked cigarettes constantly, and her breath reeked of rotting teeth and a wet ashtray. Also she had one more good reason that she would never get fired from the company, she read emails. She had the administrative password to the mail system and could read anybody's emails. The CFO of the company had her looking and reporting anything "special" thing found in other emails to him. This kept her safe.

She was next to them in the cubicle line and could hear them quite clearly. She hated the thought that Frank might be leaving them. That was bad news for her. She'd spent so much time building up her tattle-tale role with him. She couldn't lose that now! What if the new boss made her do actual programming? What would she do then?

As Frank walked over to his boss, King Jerk Face, he began to feel a little funny. He felt something in his chest. It felt like a truck was trying to park on it. He started to slow his walking pace down and began to fall. He caught himself and continued to stand but stopped walking. He was having difficulty breathing and couldn't talk. He wanted help, but when he tried to ask for it, he just couldn't. King Jerk Face's eyes widened as he stared at Frank. It was apparent to Frank his boss was not especially anxious to help him. In fact, he was moving away from him as if he was contagious.

Larry and Aaron could see something was wrong with Frank even from where they were standing. They would have run over to help sooner but were frozen shocked by what they saw. They were surprised at the sight of King Jerk Face literally jumping back away from Frank as he fell. Wow! He was even colder than Frank was. Larry could almost hear Joe saying, "I've done so much for you. Help me in my hour of need!" But his boss merely seemed to reply, "Next! Send in the next person! This one's done! Turn them and burn them." This had been one of Frank's favorite things to say to the IT crew, but it didn't seem so funny now that it was almost being used on him.

Before Larry, Aaron, or anyone else could get over there, Esther was up and by Frank's side. She gave Larry a dirty look as she ran over. She thought to herself, "Somehow he knew! Maybe he did it on purpose!"

Frank was now lying on the floor motionless. It was a scene Larry had seen many times before and knew how it would end. Esther quickly was on the phone calling 911 and asking for help, but it was pointless—Larry knew he was dead already. As Larry walked up and saw Frank's lifeless body on the floor he could no longer smell death. Wherever Frank's soul had gone, it was no longer in his body. While the rest of the people in the room questioned if life after death existed, only Frank knew for sure now. And Frank was one of those people you hoped there was a hell some kind of justice waiting for him for all the hell he put others through. In Larry's mind he wished that hell was a place where everyone had to live the lives and the consequences of people they'd mistreated on earth, feeling the pain and hurt they caused others. For Frank, this could be an eternity.

The cop was walking his beat when he heard the call go out for medical assistance. He was close to the location and knew it well. The company was known as an odd company to work for. It was a smaller company by most standards, but, in a smaller town, it stuck out. The owner had made his money by having constant road rage. He'd get cut off driving to work, so he'd pull up next to the other driver to take a photo of the person with his phone. If the person was doing something embarrassing like picking his nose, he'd post it on a website he created. It took off quickly as others began posting photos of unknowing people picking their nose. The cop had looked at the site but didn't find it to be much of a value. However, there was one photo of a lady dressed for Halloween in a Fairy Godmother outfit picking her nose at a stop light that he found very funny. But others seemed to enjoy the site and its popularity grew. He had become a web developer and started developing websites for larger corporations. He had become rich simply by taking photos of people picking their nose.

As he started to run toward the office building, the officer noticed the building had been changed. It had been upgraded with fancier tile, outside paint, and gardens. It also had some fountains and park benches. It was easy to see that some money was coming through the doors, and the owner was using some of it to impress people. He had seen this before. He was always surprised that companies never tried to impress their employees, just others in town. They never gave the employees bonuses or salary increases, but used the money for show to bring in new customers. He knew this was the case because he had seen the owner's house outside of town. The owner had rebuilt his house knowing he'd never be able to sell it. It was his "showing off" building. Most of the people in town wouldn't have been able to afford even the upkeep on the home. He knew he'd never get his money back out of it. He just wanted it to show off his wealth. In truth, if the cop had that much money, he might do the same.

As he entered the office building, he could see the crowd of workers gathering around the back of the room. They must be standing over a dead body. It was always the same. People liked to stand over the body. It was almost like they were waiting to see if it would return to life, or waiting to see the soul leave the body. Who could tell? Regardless, the cop thought it was ridiculous. As he walked closer to the body, he noticed something a bit off. He was trained to recall previous cases, as sometimes crimes are linked together. He noticed Larry was there. The cop didn't consider Larry a suspect, but it seemed odd that he was there. The cop had a flashback to all the times he'd seen Larry at the scene of someone's death.

Before the cop could get to Larry or the body, Esther stepped in front of him and said, harshly, "He said something about Frank dying before he died!" She was pointing at Larry.

The crowd around Larry split open like the Great Red Sea. Larry stood alone. Everyone in the room was standing still except for the paramedics, who had just entered the room and were working on the body. The police officer knew the paramedics had it under control and he could focus on what Esther just said.

"I'll handle this ma'am," he told her.

He walked over to Larry, pointed to an open conference room, lightly took Larry's forearm, walked him into the room, and closed the door. "Hi. I'm Detective...well, you know me. I've seen you at a lot of death scenes. It's funny how you always seem to appear when someone dies. Now, that someone was apparently your boss. Normally, I would play some mind games with you: I might ask you how your day was going or how you knew the dead person. But I don't have time for that today. So, let's cut to the chase. What's your interest in people that die? You're not killing them, are you?"

Larry stammered. "I'm not. I mean, I am. But I don't plan it that way. It just seems to happen."

So much for the easy way, the cop thought. "Okay, so we're going to do this the hard way? I'm going to take fingerprints from you and run some background checks." The officer knew that he must arrest and book Larry before he could take his fingerprints, but he also knew that Larry was probably unaware of that. "I can't hold you for now, but I will find out what's going on here. One more time. Why? This is your last chance to come clean and be honest with me." The cop thought that, if he could scare Larry, he might 'fess up. It would certainly make both of their days easier.

But Larry just stared at him for some time motionless. Finally, he replied, "Hell if I know! If you do find out, please tell me!"

The cop said nothing back. He wanted to wait and see what Larry would do. The two stood silently looking at each other, as if they were having an elementary school staring contest. The cop waited, but Larry did nothing; he just stood there waiting for the cop to say or do something else.

Larry began to wonder if he should leave the room or stay. He knew the body had been taken away by now. He could see that most of the office staff were hovering around the conference room, trying to listen in on what was being said inside. Larry just wanted this to be over with; he wanted the attention off of him. He knew he couldn't just walk out, but he wanted to. He wondered how long the two of them would stand there looking at each other waiting for one of them to speak first. What was the cop thinking?

Larry began to feel the pain in his back from a bad night's sleep and his kick out of bed. He was tired of standing, so he decided to sit down in one of the chairs.

After a minute or two, the cop finally spoke, "The funny thing is, my B.S. meter, the one that goes off in my head when someone is lying to me, is not going off now. So, either you're not lying or you're lying without even knowing it. You yourself don't understand what is going on or what you've done, somehow hidden from your conscious mind. I suspect there are two sides to you, but I'm not a psychologist. You can go for now but I'll be watching you and calling on you soon."

Larry didn't know what to say to that. He just said the first thing that popped into his mind. "Thanks, I guess."

Larry left the conference room quickly. He had not been in there for long as far as actual time spent was concerned, but it felt like forever to him. After today's events, he decided he needed a new life. One where he could feel safe, and maybe even loved. He was not really enjoying his work as a computer programmer and didn't really enjoy his home life right now with Pam. She was really getting on him about his secret.

He remembered having lunch with a co-worker, Todd. It was Todd's last day working there before taking a new job. Larry wished he'd found the job first. He wished he'd been the one leaving for a new life and a new job. On his last day of work, Todd said something that seemed weird to Larry. He said, "Once or twice a week, we've had lunch. It was the best part of my day. I'd go back to my desk, work for awhile, then go home. That was it. Our lunches were the much better than being at work with our jerk of a boss or at my home."

Larry thought that was a sad statement to make, but decided Todd was sincere. Not so for Larry. He enjoyed lunch, but that was not the best part of his day. His best part of the day was going home. He could take his time and listen to a book on tape while he drove. It wasn't far, but he drove the long way home. He told himself that it was better for the car to warm up in the winter time and to get more oil to the motor in the summer. That was his story if Pam were to ask him why it took him so long to get home from work. He would never tell that he really just wanted time by himself. Yes, he enjoyed the lunches and he understood the statement well, but Larry enjoyed his time alone more.

The cop was definitely the worst part of his day, so far. Then he remembered that his boss had just died. If Larry had not seen so many deaths, maybe that would've been the worst part of his day. He forgot about Frank. Jerk Face was dead. Larry was happy his boss was gone, but he couldn't help feeling guilty all the same. He couldn't show happy emotion, or others would pick up on his happiness and really think he had something to do with it.

As Larry walked to his desk from the conference room, he looked around. Everyone was just standing and talking. He knew they were talking about him. Larry gave a quick motion to get Aaron's attention as he walked, by but Aaron just turned his head the other way. He wanted to talk to Aaron. He had always been his sounding board, but now Aaron was giving him the cold shoulder like the others were—like others always had.

Larry always felt…different. Alien. He even felt that way with the Programmer group, which was a group of people who didn't fit other groups. Now he really felt different with Aaron punting him. As he sat down at his desk and began to think about Frank's death, Frank's boss came in and let everyone go for the day. King Jerk Face knew the employees weren't going to do any work today anyway. He might as well just send them home. At least he wouldn't have to pay the hourly employees to stand around and talk. Most of the employees walked across the street to a local bar and grill, a favorite hangout of most of the employees. They were very careful not to let Larry know where they were going. There was a typical rule when they all got together like this. The rule was, "Whoever didn't show up was fair game for being talked about." Larry didn't show up because they didn't invite him. It didn't matter whether he went or not. If they talked about him, they talked about him.

Before Larry could close down his computer, an email popped up. The message was from Pam, "Don't forget tonight. This is the address. Be there!"

After reading that message, Larry *really* wanted a new life. Pam's appointment with the hypnotist was really pushing him closer to the edge. He didn't know what to do. He looked out and saw his co-workers crossing the street, one by one. He was sure he would not be invited because he was to be the center of the conversation. They would be gossiping about what he said before Frank died. They would twist his actions until they were all one hundred percent sure that he actually caused Frank's death. Yes Frank was a jerk, but now that he had passed, he was some kind of great man in their minds. He had seen this before, and he was glad not to be part of it.

He wasn't sure what he should do for the rest of the day. At first, he just walked around town enjoying the nice weather outside. Then, he went to the local art museum. It was nothing fancy, but it was enjoyable just to walk around and stare at the art work. He'd gone with Pam a time or two, but even there she tried to control him, telling him what art he should and should not like. She had a decidedly controlling nature. To her way of thinking, Larry had to like what she liked, or they just weren't a match. And, if they weren't a match, then he didn't love her. He always found it funny that for them to match and be a good couple it was he who had a change to her taste.

The day went by surprisingly quickly. He just stood around and enjoyed the art work. If Pam knew Frank had died and Larry had the afternoon off, she would've had a big "honey-do" list for him. He hated that the purpose of the list was to keep him busy and under her thumb. She couldn't have him out, freely doing what he wanted; he might just get used to it. Larry also took a slow walk through some parks and around the ponds. He was enjoying just doing nothing. Larry was enjoying the day so much that he lost track of the time: he looked down at his watch and wondered where the day had gone. It was time to meet Pam, and he was late! He wasn't sure how it happened, but he was going to be late and she was going to be mad.

He was sure he would somehow have to pay for this or hear about it all night long.

Chapter Nine
I Pick the Holy Water

Pam arrived early in front of the house. She had planned this to make sure she beat Larry to the hypnotists. If she got there before him, she would have the upper hand. If Larry tried to back out of this, she could say she'd been waiting a long time for him and he'd have to go just because he was late. However, she wasted her time and plan because Larry was late. He knew better. He knew this was a weird form of a game for her. She was getting angrier for every minute Larry was late. He turned the corner and arrived—just over 15 minutes late. It was lucky Pam had told him to be there 20 minutes before the time they actually needed to go in and the appointment was for. She had no intention of listening to whatever excuses he had; she had a mission to get him inside to the hypnotist.

Larry walked up to Pam, knowing he was late. *This is going to be a hard sell*, he thought. *How am I going to get out of this? She's going to be downright ticked off*!" He was a programmer, not a sales person, but he'd try anyway. He started with, "Sorry I'm late. Work was really freaky and…"

Pam interrupted by stating, in a rather condescending and rude tone, "Again you're late? That's freaky for you? That must be something to… Wait! That's the same clothing you slept in! You went to work dressed in that? This looks so bad on me; it looks bad on *me* when you look such a mess. Don't you care about me? Don't you love me? Do you want me to look bad? I kicked you out of my car and made you walk home for wearing something I didn't like. You'd think you would've learned from that."

Larry figured he'd give it one more attempt to cool her jets and said, "I was late because of work, because…"

Pam cut him off again, "Yeah, yeah, yeah. Let's just go inside and see what the hypnotist can do for you."

Larry changed his focus from trying to get out of trouble to maybe trying to get out of this appointment. He was disturbed by her phrase, "What the hypnotist can do for you." He really didn't like the idea of getting hypnotized in the first place, and he thought it was unfair that he would be the only one hypnotized. He had asked Pam earlier in the week when she set up the appointment if she was also getting hypnotized. She only answered, "Larry, why would I get hypnotized? I don't have anything wrong with me other than the fact that I'm married to you! I'm just trying to help you be normal. I don't freak out going down the street when I see people!"

Pam marched on in the hypnotist office, and he followed her inside like a puppy going to the vet. The building was in an older part of town, and the place obviously had once been someone's home. It was on a busy street, and most of the houses on the street had now been converted into some type of business office. The basement of the building and second floor had been converted to apartments, and the first floor was given over to the business.

Larry noticed the "For Rent" sign in the window of the door of the basement apartment. He had rented a basement apartment once and hated it. It always seemed cold, and the sewer backed up way too often. He was glad he didn't have to live in one anymore. Besides if he lived in basement apartment with Pam, he would never hear the end of her complaining about the place. Larry also noticed a similar structure with an apartment in the basement for rent across the street from the hypnotist's house. But that main floor office was occupied by an

Indian shaman. Hopefully, Pam didn't know about him or he would be the next stop.

Pam and Larry walked into the waiting room, which had been, at one time, the great room of the house. Nobody was there—just an empty desk set up to look like a receptionist's desk. The desk clearly had never been used for that function. No receptionist had ever been hired because apparently business had never taken off and required one. Some would call this a mom and pop business, but it was still missing half of that business model. Larry was hoping Pam had made a mistake and somehow gotten the appointment date wrong. Just as he was about to say to Pam that this might be the wrong night, a voice came from the back of the house. It was a man's voice that somehow had a reassuring tone. The voice said, "I'll be right out. Please take a seat." Larry looked around for a seat to take but only saw two Goodwill chairs lined against the wall. In fact, the chairs were so poorly held together from years of use,

Larry was sure that Goodwill would not even take them.

Pam had high hopes of getting Larry well with the hypnotist. She wanted him "fixed now." Well, really it was whatever she wanted to call it at the time. Tonight, it was "getting Larry well." Tomorrow night it might be called "stop the freak show that he did."

Pam had one last chance to tell Larry not to mess it up, so she quietly leaned over toward him and whispered, "Now, no weird stuff. You're going to try this, correct?" Pam moved her head up and down, showing him how to nod in the same way you'd treat a little kid. She was making sure that he knew that "Yes" was the only option he really had. In the past, she'd nod like this until he'd agree with her. Pam could see in his eyes that he was going to fight this a little, but that was okay with her as long as he finally agreed. What fun would it be for her if he did everything without at least a little fight?

Not always fun to get your way if you don't have to fight for it first.

Before she could get him to agree and fully submit to her will, the hypnotist walked into the room. Pam stopped nodding, not wanting the hypnotist to see her game. She didn't want someone else seeing how much she patronized Larry. The hypnotist was not what Pam expected. He wasn't a very impressive man by his looks. Pam hoped his skill level was more impressive than his appearance. People always told her that she couldn't judge a book by the cover, but in her opinion that was the best way to judge somebody.

As the hypnotist approached, he began to look them over, very slowly, one at a time. He had seen and worked with a number of couples and could quickly size them up. Already, he could see this couple was going to be hard to work with. He heard the conversation that they were having before he entered the room. He decided to enter the room when he did to help the young man before his wife pinned him down. Pam looked and acted like her friend, Jen. Jen had referred the hypnotist to Pam because she thought he was helpful to her and her husband. She knew Larry and figured the hypnotist could work wonders for them also.

The hypnotist recalled how Jen was always thinking it was some other person's fault or issue, when really she was her own problem. The hypnotist hated working with Jen and her husband. Jen made him work on her husband, slowly twisting and contorting his thoughts until he finally understood what he was doing. Lucky for him, he also had problems. This was tricky for the hypnotist. Typically, couples didn't want to be there. They didn't want to change. Change is a funny concept. It's usually a good thing, unless you are doing the changing. When others are changing to make your life better, that's easy. But for someone to change him or herself to make life better, that's hard. So when Jen and Pam said they wanted help, they wanted the hypnotist to change their husbands to better fit their life style. Kind of like taking a cat in to be declawed. The hypnotist often wondered why the couples with whom he had the most problems always had friends in the same position coming to him. They just seemed to run in packs; maybe they attracted each other or heard someone at work going on about her husband and found common ground. But whatever it was that pulled them together, after one found him, his business took off. In a way, he felt like the vet neutering a dog; he did it to make a living, but he felt for each one he did it to. Well it was time for his next dog to be fixed.

He sighed, silently. It was time to get started.

He said, "Please, please. Come back to my office."

They both walked back to what was once a dining room. It was a mildly lit room with chairs that seemed to say "sit and take a load off your feet." They were the type of chairs you sank into. The kind that felt good sitting and relaxing in. The room looked like a doctor's office that had been hit by an old VW bus from the 60s. It had been decorated oddly, with some of the 70s or 80s stuff from the new age movement that added to the 60s vibe. Larry knew that this doctor, if he was a real doctor, must have done some weird stuff in the 60s.

As they entered the room, the hypnotist asked, "How can I help both of you today?" He made sure to use the word "both," as in "*both* of you," while he privately added, "and not just him." He knew where it would go, but he would try to help both, if he could.

Before he could say anything else, Pam jumped in. "We've been having problems...or, I should say, Larry is having problems...that impact our marriage. You've helped some of our friends, so I thought you could also help us." Pam kept it short; what else was there to say, but "fix him now"?

The hypnotist felt he already knew what the real issue was and answered carefully. After all, it was a big part of his job to get the couple down the path walking toward their own solution, not just telling them the answer. However, the couple had to be ready for that. So he started with his typical general questions.

"Oh, so is it something in the bedroom, love life, talking skills, money, or a past event?" he asked, with a very slight pause between his suggestions. This four covered most true problems. He knew by Pam's fake smile that she did not care about true problems; she just wanted him fixed.

Pam continued to do all the talking.

"You could say it was something in the head-room!" Pam gave a little half smirk immediately after she said that. She quickly looked at the hypnotist to see if he caught her little joke. The hypnotist knew not to react, so Pam continued, "Larry has this weird thing he does that pushes people off. We need help understanding it and why he does it. I have asked him to talk about it, but he won't."

Maybe it's simply you pushing people off, not him! I can already tell you are a self righteous bitch! Of course, that's not what he said. It was not a gift sometimes to so easily see and understand people, but he had this gift all his life. It was especially trying on him when he had to read people whose thoughts leaned on the side of evil thoughts over good. Like Pam.

He calmly stated in a practiced monotone, as if he had not heard her, "So, this is how it works: we assess each person by themselves. Both of you are going to go under, and then…"

Pam abruptly interrupted and aggressively said, "No! Just Larry. He freaks out on some people. Most of the time, he doesn't even know them. And truthfully, I want it to stop right now. I told you, I'm fine. Larry is not. We are here so you can fix him." She thought to herself, *wow, this guy can't take a hint. If he still doesn't get it, we're out of here, and I better get my money back.*

The hypnotist knew it was definitely time to get Pam out of the room. In that practiced, level monotone, he purred, "Okay. Pam, can you step outside? I need to work one-on-one with Larry. That works best. But, after our session, I still want to work with you."

Pam flinched like someone dodging a punch and loudly stated, "I don't think so! I said I'm fine. I told you to fix *him*. Do it!" She stormed out of the room before the hypnotist could say anything else, making sure she had the last word. It wouldn't have mattered, though. He knew that anything he said wouldn't be heard by her anyway. She had made up her mind what she wanted, and her type would not stop until she got it, even if it was the death of her or someone else.

The hypnotist was waiting for Pam to get out of hearing range. He was, after all, not in the business of angering with his customers. He didn't want to say anything that would potentially cost him future business. He also knew what Pam wanted. She wanted to hear him belittle Larry and get to the root cause of why he got "freaked out" around some people. Instead, the hypnotist closed the door and tried to get Larry to unwind a bit before attempting to help him. He needed him to relax and not be so stressed out from Pam's outbursts. He could see how Larry was on edge with her present. *Time to lighten it up a little*, he thought.

The hypnotist waited for what seemed like an hour before saying anything to Larry. In reality, it was only a couple of minutes. It was just Larry and the hypnotist in the room now. The room had grown bigger and less pushy now that Pam had walked out. Both just wanted time to enjoy it.

In a conversational tone of voice, tinged with a bit of excitement, the hypnotist said, "Well, first we'll help you, Larry! Then, maybe we can work on Pam's control-freak issues."

Larry laughed and started to smile a little. He could actually feel himself start to relax. The hypnotist knew he would. After all, that's how he made his living. He had the gift of understanding how to make people feel at home, even when they felt uneasy. As Larry began to relax on the couch, he knew it was time to see if he could really help this young man. He quietly launched into his hypnosis routine, softly dragging out each word.

"Okay…good. Now that I got you to finally relax, all you need to do is listen to my voice. Let the anxiety and aggression of the day wash away. Let go of all that stuff. All you have to do is just listen to my voice. As you do, you'll go deeper and deeper into sleep."

Larry slowly looked more and more tired as the hypnotist continued to talk. His eyelids closed, and his head drooped. Larry was relaxing and falling further and further under the hypnotic spell.

The hypnotist left Larry in the deep sleep for a couple of minutes, allowing him to truly have some rest. He found this best; his patients felt so much better afterwards.

The hypnotist asked, "Larry, how do you feel?"

Larry simply replied, "Good."

The hypnotist loved asking questions when people were under. He even asked questions that maybe he should not have asked, as they didn't pertain to why the person was there in the first place. He figured the patient wouldn't remember anyway, so why not? He felt it was one of the perks of the job—and sometimes it actually led him to a diagnosis. He once asked a lady why she ate so much. He was shocked when she told him she didn't want to have sex with her husband so she put on enough weight to get him disgusted at her and not wanting to be with her. She had grown sick of him and hated his touch. The fatter she got, the less he wanted to touch her; it had worked. The hypnotist had to work for months to get her to slowly understand why she was morbidly obese. Once she finally figured it out, she divorced her husband and lost 150 pounds.

Now, the hypnotist asked Larry, "Larry, do you love Pam?"

Larry sleepily responded, "Yes, I do."

Without contemplating Larry's response, he asked, "Do you happily love Pam? Do you think she is mean to you?"

Larry again replied sleepily, "I can't get anybody else. I'm too weird. Everyone knows it, but she puts up with me."

The hypnotist saw that this was going somewhere, so he felt compelled to drive further into the discussion. He asked, "Larry, why do you feel you're so weird? Speak freely and without feeling. Just tell me what's on your mind."

Larry muttered, "I am because of who I am. I am because of who my dad is. I am his son, and the son must do what the father does. It's part of me. It's the part of me I keep hidden even from myself. It's the dark side of me that is closing in, taking over all of me. Each day it comes closer to taking me over completely."

This was not the first time the hypnotist had heard someone state something like this under hypnosis. He knew there was some underlying meaning behind it. In this case, he knew Larry had never had his father around, so it must be something related to that.

He told Larry, "Larry, you are who you are. You are exactly what you've made of yourself. You are a product of you, not what your family did or who they were. We each form our own life. We are a product of what we do."

Larry opened his eyes. His eyes where back, but not kind as before. He did not appear to be aware or conscious, but the look his eyes portrayed was a look of pure evil. A cold shiver ran down the hypnotist's spine. It was as if someone had taken a handful of ice and forced it down his naked back. Larry raised his head toward the hypnotist's face, his eyes emotionless and empty. He answered the question in a monotone, but his voice conveyed annoyance.

"My dad did more than skip out when I was young—and soon it will be my turn. You are in danger asking me these questions! Our path, the path I must take, it's who I am, who my dad was, and who I am. Not all people have a path, but I do. I must do my father's work."

Larry looked even colder and more emotionless now. Not blinking, not moving, waiting to see what the hypnotist did next. His eye color changed to almost a perfect black. He never blinked, and his breathing was very slow. He didn't move or make a sound. The hypnotist looked him over from head to toe and began to question his personal safety. Though his patients typically were in a semi-vegetative state during their sessions, sometimes they'd have physical reactions. He was used to that. But this was very different than anything else he'd ever seen. It was much more evil. Quite frankly, it scared the shit out of him. He couldn't talk. He couldn't ask any more questions, though he wanted to. But he understood the warning…

Larry broke the silence and in a whisper said, "I am the words many are scared to say. Do you want me to say them? It will change your life forever. It is the same word you wouldn't say when you were a little boy. Do you recall when you fell in that well and almost... "

The hypnotist interrupted Larry because he really didn't want him to finish that statement. He stammered out the words, "No, no, Larry. Please, close your eyes and relax. We have no need to go there. Slowly go to sleep and calm down."

He breathed a sigh of relief as Larry calmed down and placed his head back leaned his head back against the couch, slowly closing his eyes.

"Okay. Now you're going to awaken on the count of five. You will feel fine and not remember any of what we talked about. You will feel great. One, you're coming around.

Two, all the memory of this is going away. Three, you will not come back to visit me again. Four, Pam's mean words will not harm your spirit or hurt your feelings ever again. Five, you're feeling great, and you're awake."

Larry opened his eyes. They were again their normal color, and he looked more like himself. Kind, meek eyes that showed years of being hurt and hen pecked by his wife. The hypnotist took special note to make sure Larry didn't look like he was still possessed by a hell hound. Larry really didn't have a warm look to him, but pale looked normal for Larry. It was a relief to observe Larry's regular demeanor. The hypnotist, still visibly shaking over the frightening ordeal, began to feel wetness in his pants. He didn't want to let Larry see he'd wet himself, so he covered himself with his notebook. At this point, he just wanted Larry out of his office and gone forever. He never wanted to see him again.

Larry slowly awakened. He woke with a funny feeling. He knew he had just been hypnotized as the time on the clock had jumped ahead. He couldn't remember being under nor what he said when he was under, but, by the way the hypnotist was acting, he began to wonder what he had said. The hypnotist wasn't looking Larry in the eyes and was standing in a very odd position. Larry could tell the hypnotist just wanted Larry out of his room and gone.

Larry figured he'd break the ice and said, "Wow! I feel great! How did it go?" The hypnotist hesitated and almost said, "bad," but didn't. He thought twice about it, as he knew his answer would only bring more questions. And he just wanted Larry gone and out of his office. He also wanted Larry's annoying wife gone and out of his life as well. So, after thinking carefully about his answer, he just smiled and said, "Good! Really good! We are all still here and good! No need for you to come back. I found out that it all ties back to your father leaving at an early age. Everything is fixed now." He stopped smiling and began to motion for Larry to get out.

He helped Larry off the couch, opened the door to his office, and began urging Larry to the front door. Pam saw them coming and, in her typical Pam fashion, got right in the way so Larry couldn't pass by. The hypnotist thought to himself, *Shit*! *Here comes Toto, Larry's little doggy, to bark and yelp at me*.

Pam asked, "How did it go? Is he fixed?"

How can you fix evil? That thought quickly vanished, as his new goal was to get them the hell out of his office. He answered Pam: "This is not a vet's, where you take your dog to get fixed, but he is good. There is no need to come back. Oh, and by the way, this one is on the house. Let's just call this a peace offering." He hoped that by being short with

Pam it would push her hot button, piss her off, and she'd get out thinking he was just a jerk.

As he urged Larry to the front door, Pam stepped in the way again, obviously not liking what the hypnotist said. Pam asked, "Peace offering? What d'ya mean? Just tell me, will he stop doing weird stuff around people?" The hypnotist decided to simply snap at her again, hoping it would anger her so she'd take her husband home and never come back.

"Only time will tell. If he doesn't, you might want to try someone else. I did all I could do. Well, it's time to go; close up shop for the night; time to get home and feed grandma."

This got her. Pam was shocked and flustered, and, while he had both of them on the run, he pushed the pair out of the door and shut it behind them, turning off the OPEN light in the window. He fell against the closed door, breathing hard. Now he could feel himself shaking a little less. He looked up to the heavens and spoke aloud. "Please do not let him come back…" He continued as he locked the door, "Some doors should not be opened, aren't safe to be opened. We all have a dark side that we hide, but he has a killer one. Wow!" He was very happy they had left.

Now standing outside, like a drunk just coming down from his buzz and trying his wits so he can find his way home, Larry was being attached with sharp words from oh so loving wife Pam. She wanted to know what happened in back room after she stepped out, why the hypnotist had toss them out, but somehow, this time, the questions did not get under his skin as much. Larry thought the hypnosis must have helped that. He was ready to go back in again for more if that was the outcome, until he saw the OPEN light go off in the window and a feeling come over him—he never cared to go back. But he knew he had to answer Pam, so he spoke, "I don't know. I can't remember anything, but I feel good. I feel really good. Do you want to go do something?

Pam was not happy with this answer at all; she had had high hopes for much more tonight. She had thought he would come out in tears, not happy; in tears from feeling bad for doing this to her and others. He would have great remorse for making her ashamed of him and his smelling thing. She had envisioned how he would fall at her feet and ask forgiveness for his sins—not be happy and in a good mood. That was not her plan! Did they just have a party back in that room? What the hell went on in there? With this thought, she asked, "Is it, you *can't* remember or don't *want* to remember? Are you just being closed mouth about this like your smelling thing?"

Larry gave her a look that said, "What are you talking about?

Before he could say the words, she added, "You heard me! Well, I have a backup plan. I thought you might snowball him or something, so tomorrow night we are going to a Native American shaman and see what he says. Besides this clown didn't charge us, so we can afford extra time with shaman as well."

Larry had never heard of a shaman before. What was that? He remembered seeing some old western movies that had a shaman— that can't be it. Again before he could ask, Pam filled him in. "A shaman is a Native American spirit man, someone who will pull out your inner person and find our problems. Help you down the road as a spiral guide." Pam paused then spoke angrily. "Oh yeah, and fix your weird crap so I can stand to live with you!"

Wow, she had this all thought out. What would be next? He had read once in a book that women marry men for what they can make out of them, and men marry the women for who she is at the time. Pam had made a lot of changes to him, but still had big plans. She had given up on many of the tasks she did in her life—she was lazy and ran out of energy. But for the task of changing Larry, she had unlimited energy.

"Pam," Larry asked, "Okay, so what if that does not work?"

Pam did not know what to say. She was out of options, so she felt it was time to let him know that the next one better work or else. This was it.

"Then I toss you in holy water and cast out this demon or burn you at the stake—I don't know which yet. Maybe just lock you up inside and away from people. Still looking into my options."

Larry was still in a good mood from the hypnosis. He was feeling fine, and her words did not hurt as much tonight. He decided to joke with her. "I pick the holy water."

Pam was clearly upset now, mad as a wet hen. "Not funny!" she replied. "I'll email you the address of the shaman. And I want you to be at his house tomorrow night *on time*. Now let's go get something to eat, I'm hungry. And don't be late tomorrow."

They walked off down the road together to find a place to eat. Neither was talking much or noticing that some of the street lights they past kicked off after they walked by. Both were too busy in their own minds to notice or talk to the other person. Clearly, Pam was still upset, but Larry seemed oblivious to her mood. Larry was in one of the best moods of his life, feeling like he wanted to do everything tonight and enjoy it all as if it was his last days of living.

Chapter Ten
Time to Kick it Up a Notch

The next night was much like the night before for Larry. In the crisp fall air, you could almost feel the kids' energy building toward the upcoming magical night when kids would go door to door and ask for candy. Larry was still in a good mood from the night before, not as euphoric, but still in higher sprits than usual. Maybe it was that feeling in the air—the anticipation of the coming night, Halloween. He did love that holiday. He really loved the smell of the burning candles in pumpkins and dressing up. Pam never liked dressing up. She would reluctantly do it from time to time, if he made a lot of promises to her. This year he wouldn't even go down that road. It was just too much work trying to get her to dress up also, and he enjoyed it much more without having to deal with her or her complaints about her hair or whatever. She could just stay home, and he would go out to the clubs by himself. Maybe he could go with his coworkers.

As Larry walked up to the address Pam had given him for the shaman's house, he saw her standing outside the door. He could tell by the look on her face that she was already upset with him. She was going to work him over again.

Wow, she really likes getting worked up about things, he thought to himself. He would try starting it off with a joke and lighten it up. But before he could get anything out of his mouth, Pam barked out, "You're late for the shaman! I told you not to be late, and you're almost three minutes late." Larry knew he was not late. Pam had all her clocks, including her watch, set five minutes fast, so she would never be late. The problem with that was that everyone else was late by her time, and her time was the correct time—in her mind. He thought he would point this out and try to clear his name. Pam thought if she kept confessing others' sins, somehow that would get her into heaven.

Larry spoke. "You set your watch fast five minutes, and…" But before he could finish what he was saying, she cut him off again, as if to say that what he had to say was not important to her, nor would ever be. So just drop it.

She barked, "Yeah, anyway. You're not going to freak out on this Indian shaman, are you? Don't do your smelling freaking out stuff. Not tonight, not this night. I want to hear what he has to say about us. He could really help you—and us. If I could just get you fixed, we would be good…it would be perfect."

"We would be good"—this phrase rang in his head. If she did not feel good about them, then why marry him in the first place? What was this rush lately to "get him fixed," as if she were on some kind of deadline or something. He knew she was pushy and wanted her way, but she was really pushing now. He did not feel like bringing this up; he still had not gotten his first point made, so he just added, "Not a problem...so again, back to what I was saying, almost three minutes late is not really... "

But again she cut him off. "Whatever, whatever! Let's go inside already."

Today Larry felt a little different. Today he felt like trying to make his point. He was not sure what had happened last night at the hypnotist's, but he somehow felt more sure of himself.

Pam was not in the mood for one of Larry's "I'm going to get you to listen to me" stands. He seemed ready to push it more today than he ever had in the past. She wasn't sure why; she had given the signals to stop it and listen to her. But tonight he kept on with it: her watch was fast, yeah, we know that, but she was not going to say, "You're really not late, and I'm mad for no reason." Okay, she was just pissed, she thought to herself. She needed a reason, and so she'd stick to his being late. Before he could comment again, Pam grabbed his arm and ran both of them up to the front door and knocked. An older woman opened the door and let them in. She seemed friendly but yet stand-offish—probably just doing her job, although Pam could not tell if she was part of the shaman's family or if she was an employee. She tried to figure it out. She wondered how much money the shaman made—not much; the house was old. It did have an apartment for rent under it; she had seen the sign in the front window as she was waiting for Larry.

The woman was now showing them into an outdoor sitting area. It was open to the sky, but not open to the street. It was clearly set up so that you could not been seen by others driving or walking by. In the middle of this space was a large fire pit with colorful fire burning. And sitting by it was an older man, waving an eagle's feather, tossing some items into the fire, and clearing the air with the feather. Each time he tossed something into the fire, the color of the fire would change. He was chanting words that neither Larry nor Pam understood. Their guide left without a word, and, standing back out of his sight, Pam and Larry realized that this older man must be the shaman. His clothing made him look like he walked out of an old western movie but stopped by a second-hand store and added some items before getting here. His eyes where full of life, but his body had lost some of its life.

The shaman was busy, but he stopped as if something was out of place. As if someone or something had pinched his soul. Unsure, he looked around him, trying to find what was upsetting his sprit. He could feel something, something dark in the general area with him. Out of the corner of his eye he spotted Pam and Larry, standing by the entrance. He had known clients were coming, but he was puzzled about them and his feeling. Surely this could not be them. He felt a really dark spirit he did not need or want here. As he looked over to tell the two of them that he needed to clear the air of this darkness, he noticed the dark spirit was coming from Larry. This discovery made him jump with fear. But how could this be? How could a man hold this spirit? Who was he here for—could it be himself? The shaman had to find out but more, but he had to do it safely.

"Which one are you here for, me or her?" he asked Larry.

Pam jerked her head and looked at Larry. *Was he doing his weird look or smell thing again? He had better not be weirding out again, the jerk.* Pam turned to yell at Larry and tell him to stop when she noticed that Larry was just standing still, more in shock than anything, eyes locked with the shaman. Now, it seemed, she had found someone weirder than Larry. It was time to get back on track and get it to the reason they had come to see him. She was not going to pay for something she did not ask for, no matter how much it might help Larry. In an attempt to put things right, she said, "I brought him here. He's my husband. I want to see if you can help us."

The shaman saw the lady named Pam touch the dark spirit that she called husband, and say that she had brought him. Somehow, she controlled him. How could she do that to so dark of a spirit? How could she say that she brought him? No human could touch a dark sprit or tell him where to go and when. And she could see him! Only the paranormal could see dark spirits. He had to ask, "You can see him? You hear him?" as he pointed to Larry in disbelief.

Pam knew this older man would be strange, being a shaman and all, but asking if she could she see and hear her husband was off the wall! And she had thought she had seen it all, being married to Larry. Admittedly, there were times she did not want to see him, like when he was being so weird. But…

He's an older man, she thought, before saying, "Yes, why wouldn't I? He's my husband. I don't want to hear or see him sometimes, but that's another story and partly why we are here." She paused. "I thought I would get to ask the questions," she added rather brusquely. She thought she would wake this older man up by snapping her fingers back and forth, before she would waste any more breath, "Let's stay on track here, old man."

The shaman grabbed some dust from his special pile, the pile he kept just in case of times like this. This was certainly one of those one in a million times that he needed it. Quickly he tossed it into the fire, and the flames changed to a bluish color. The fire sounded as if it screamed with the color change, and as the color died down so did the sounds that seem to be screams. The shaman leaned into sounds of the fire for protection from Larry. He was safe from this dark sprit, but for just a short time. He was not sure for how long. He needed to get them out of his house before the protection wore off. He was stressed. It was a matter of death or life; he needed them out fast and without delay. But he needed to know something first.

"Ma'am," he said, looking at Pam, "You do not know what fire and power you toy with. If you are married to this man, that is what keeps you safe and unburned from the fires that burn forever. And the dark smell of the woods cannot circle you. Many of us do not know how we are protected until the protection is removed. You would be wise to shine your protection shield and not try to crack holes in it." Again he tossed some dust into the fire and leaned into the smoke coming off the fire.

Okay, that's it; he's off his rocker! We have a winner in being weirder than Larry, I did not think I could find one, but I did, Pam thought to herself. *I need to get him back on track again.*

Aloud, she said rudely, "Yeah, yeah...shield...got it! I'm good at cleaning. That's great, but now can I ask my question? I thought *he* was weird, but you take the cake."

Now Pam could see the shaman was growing angry and not wanting to talk. He made that feeling plain by stating forcefully, "You are allowed one question. That was it. NO, you cannot ask more, so now you must both go. Go now! I can't tell you anything, but please go now, and do not come back. I can't tell you why, but, each second you spend here, we are all in danger. Go now. Go before the dark smell of the woods comes to call. I have many questions also, but no time for them. But time has ran out."

Larry had stood back and watched this interaction between the shaman and Pam, like watching a play unfold in front of him. Funny thing, he was not doing anything, no weird smells, nothing at all. But this shaman was freaking out, and Pam was on his case for it, just as she was with Larry when he "freaked out." He thought it was kind of nice to see her on someone else's back for a change. Sure, he felt sorry for the shaman, but it was a pleasant break for himself. It reminded him of when he was in school and the bullies would pick on some other kid for the day; it was just a relief it was not him for a change. Yes, he felt sorry for the other kid, but really the break was nice. He had to thank the shaman somehow. Maybe a handshake and a thank you would do?

Larry went to shake his hand and added, "Sorry, sir, for taking up your time."

At this, the shaman jumped back, with even more alacrity than he had before. He could not touch this man! He could never get that dark sprit out then. He just needed him to leave! What did he have to do to get them to leave and leave now?

He tried once more. "No! You must not touch anybody but your wife; she is safe from it. The dark smell of the woods grows in you, and it is growing fast. Leave now. It will find you soon. That is what you smell on others, the dark smell of the old woods."

It occurred to Larry that the older man was acting weird, but maybe he knew something. It was time to find out. "Am I going to die?" he asked the older man.

"Someone else can smell something—on *you,* Larry; how funny," Pam cried out.

But the shaman did not find it funny. He had warned her to take care of Larry, or else. Now he just wanted them to leave.

"No, he does not smell of death; that is not why the dark smell of the woods comes for you. He will come. He watches you, waiting for the right time and place. My fire keeps us safe now, but not for long. The dark smell of the woods can only be slowed, not stopped. It will find you. As a mother must find her child, it will come after you. Nothing will stop it; now leave me."

Perhaps giving a first sign of caring for Larry, Pam was not sure what to say after that. But she still felt the need to ask something, so she asked the shaman, "Should I take him to a doctor?   Or should I take both of you?"

She does not understand, thought the shaman, but he did not have the time nor care to explain more to her. She was thick-headed and would not listen to him anyway. He wanted them gone. *Couldn't she take the hint? Time to move from hinting to telling them. Time to kick it up a notch.*

"No, what you call 'doctor' cannot help him; it's not of this place or time It lives in the place that you only see when you turn your head really fast and glimpse out of the corner of your eye. For a split second you see it, and it makes you dizzy." He tossed more items on the fire. "Leave now, I feel the dark wood's wind screaming its anger that you are here, and I've said too much. Run, now..."

Pam was not sure what was going on. She just knew he wanted them out of his place, and she now thought that was a good idea. Besides, if she left now, she might not have to pay him. She turned to grip Larry's arm and "exit stage left," but Larry was already heading for the door and leaving her behind. What a shock! But she would have time later to ask him why he did this. For now, she just wanted out. Her spider sense was going off, telling her to leave.

As they exited the house and stepped back into the street, Pam started to question Larry.

"What the hell was that all about? Oh, you're not going to tell me? Ah, I guess I'll just forget it—and *you*!"

She had had it. The whole thing was just too weird. And he had left her behind in there. Now it was time for her to ditch him. She took off in a huff, letting Larry know by her look that he was not to follow her. Out of the corner of her eye, she could see wisps of different colors of smoke from the fire, curling above the house top of the old man. The older man was still at work, doing whatever he did in the back yard. *A weirder old man, I'll never know*, she thought.

Larry was standing by himself, not sure where to go. He could tell the shaman didn't want him back in his house or close to him. Pam didn't want him to follow her home either. What was he supposed to do? He decided he would take a slow walk home and just enjoy the fresh air. Soon it would be too cold for that, so he would go by the old maxim: "better enjoy it while you can; you never know when it will be gone."

Pam was right that the episode was weird, very weird. He now knew how others felt about him freaking out over them, when he could smell them. Maybe that was the purpose of this evening; maybe this had all been planned, just to show him. No, if that were true, if Pam had planned it, she would have brought along one or more of her friends; they would have also enjoyed telling him he was weird. She would have made some kind of party out of it.

Chapter Eleven
The Secret Comes Out

Larry used a lot of time to walk home that night. He took the long way; then took it again. He did not have to work in the morning; it was Saturday, so he could stay up later. He had a lot of thinking to do. A lot was said by the shaman, and it was kind of like drinking from a fire hose, too much at one time to make heads or tails out of it. He also thought about happier times as a kid: those times you keep playing back in your mind when times are hard. Those times that seem to grow fewer as you get older.

He also thought about telling Pam why he jumped out of the way of some people. She really wanted to know, and maybe it was time to tell her. The worst she could do would be mean to him; yell at him. She did that a lot, so that was nothing new. She could leave him. That was it, the key thing she held over his head: she could leave him. This is what really scared him. He didn't know if he could find someone else to put up with his eccentricities. Pam was his only hope, his only chance of growing old with someone, his only chance at having a normal life.

It's time to tell her, he decided as he walked up the street to his house. He just had to walk inside and tell her. As he walked up to the front door, he could hear her inside, moving things around, as she did when she was mad. The more upset she was over something, the more the house was rearranged. He opened the door. She had to be very upset, as most of the items he could see had been relocated. She saw him as she was pushing a chair into her wanted location. She abruptly turned, heading for the back room of the apartment, so he could not talk to her.

"Wait, Pam! Pam, just wait. I'll tell you what you want to know. But just remember that

I'm telling you this because you asked, not that I want to. You win."

Pam stopped and turned around. He had never seen her stop so quickly to listen to him before. He supposed there was a first time for everything. Maybe things would change after he told her. Maybe things would be better. Or maybe she would feel that this was the last straw. Maybe she would leave him. Either way, he had to give it a try.

"This is your last chance to say no Pam. We can never go back to what we had before once you hear what I'm about to tell you," Larry began slowly, waiting for her to interrupt him as usual. When she didn't, he continued. "You'll never view me the same way again. Are you sure you want that? It's like when you were a kid and found out about nuclear bombs. You suddenly realized that live can be gone in a flash. You never really feel safe again. Are you sure you want that?"

Her face lit up. Of course she wanted to know. She had been pestering him for years about this, hadn't she? He waited for her answer. She was still, and then she said quietly, "I must know. And stop being so overdramatic. Nothing could be that big. You make it sound like I'll leave you or something. I'm not leaving you to find someone else." She smiled and added, "I don't want you to mess up their life, so tell me."

This was more like the Pam he knew, the Pam he loved and hated. She always had a comment to add, like a knife in the back. She had to make sure that he would feel badly about himself. No one would ever feel better about themselves because of something she said.

How to start; how to start? He couldn't decide. Pam just stood there, waiting for him to talk. After waiting patiently for about a half a second, she started making faces, as if to say, "go ahead already, now, anytime…"

Larry looked around the room, pondering how to explain it. It was like telling someone about the ocean when she had never seen it.

Just then their cat walked in the room and jumped on the chair next to Larry. Suddenly, he knew how to tell her. Actually, he *smelled* how to tell her.

"Here, take the cat," he urged Pam, shoving the cat into her arms. "Do you smell anything on him? Do you?"

Pam gave Larry an aggravated look, but eventually sniffed the cat. She was not sure what this had to do with what he was going to tell her, but she would play along for now but he better get to the point soon. "It smells like a cat, Larry." She handed the cat back to him.

Larry backed away, as if the cat had been sprayed by a skunk. And, to him, it did smell that way. Larry was certain their dear pet was going to die soon.

Larry put the cat down, but it kept walking around his legs. He looked at Pam.

"You smell a cat. But I smell something more. Others don't seem to smell it, but it's so over-powering to me. It's like someone poured dead rotting leaves on the cat. It's a horrible smell." Larry paused. "And I smell it on people sometimes too."

"Okay," Pam said slowly. "You smell things. Things other people can't. But what does it all mean?"

"I don't exactly know," Larry replied. "I don't know anybody else that has this talent. I never got to know my dad, or his family, so I don't know if he could."

Pam knew he was telling the truth about this. She could easily tell when he was lying, as he was no good at it. It aroused her interest even more. What was it all about, the smell? She had a ton of questions, and it was time to ask. Her mind was racing. "Well, what *does* it smell like?"

"Maybe…hell?" Larry offered.

This only made her think of more questions. She was asking them fast now, not even giving him time to answer them before more were popping up in her head and out of her mouth.

She found out that his nose burned or tingled when he smelled the smell—like when you dive into a pool and breathe in chlorine water. She learned that, as the person drew closer to the end of their time, the smell grew stronger. It hurt his nose and body to be close to someone who was about to die. It became too much to take, and that was why he couldn't stand being next to someone with that smell. The stench was just too much.

All of Larry's abnormal, awkward social skills seemed to make sense now. She was not sure if he was actually smelling death. But the key was that *he* believed he was, and that was why he behaved strangely. Larry also explained that not everyone smelled the same. There were two distinct smells, one sweet and one sour. Both stunk, but each was tinged with a different aroma.

Pam started to consider a new angle. Wow, to smell someone that was going to die— what power! If they knew someone was going to die, she could take a life insurance policy out on him. Then, the money could be theirs! But of course, they could only do this one or two times before the insurance companies would catch on. Maybe they could get some insurance on their cat. Their cat! Oh crap! Was Larry saying that their cat was going to die? She had had that cat since before they got married. She looked down at the cat, still rubbing up against Larry's legs. He looked fine. Smokey wasn't dying. Larry had to be full of it.

"Like you *know*! You're weird and cracked if you think I'm going to buy this stuff. You can't smell death. Look at Smokey. He's fine. If he stinks so badly, then why isn't he acting like he's dying?"

Larry had been waiting for this to set in. Pam had had a lot of questions about death and smelling death, but she had overlooked the fact that the cat had the smell. She had now come to that realization: for him to be correct and telling the truth was to say that the cat would also die. He had to tell her.

"He is dying, Pam. From what I can smell, he only has a couple of days left. Well, at best guess, and that's all I can do. But just a couple of days before he..."

"Smokey isn't dying!" Pam shouted. "You've never liked him! I bet you're going to do something to him just to prove your stupid point!"

Pam picked up Smokey, threw open their apartment door, and strode over to the apartment across the hall. She knocked loudly, as if she was running from a serial killer. All the while, she was stroking and petting Smokey, and shooting furrowed glances back at Larry.

Their neighbor, Cindy, answered the door, dressed in a house coat and slippers. She was an older woman who spent most of her days looking after her cat, Clarabelle. Sometimes she looked after Smokey. She had few visitors, and Pam really only stopped by when she needed something. Cindy missed the days when she "had a life," with family to care for and good friends to talk to. Her husband had passed away and her kids didn't visit anymore. She felt she was just waiting for it to all end or somehow get better. Pam was a moody person, she thought, but she helped her out. Maybe because she had nothing better to do, or maybe because she was trying to make up for things she had done when she was younger. Or just maybe she felt sorry for Smokey.

"Hi, Pam," Cindy said, and then, looking past her, "Hi, Larry." She turned her gaze to the cat in Pam's arms. "Hi, Smokey! I take it Smokey wants to play with Clarabelle?"

No, Pam thought to herself, *he wants to live*! But how do you tell that to someone?

"Yes, please. We need to run out for a bit. Would you watch Smokey…" she looked back at Larry, " …and make sure nothing happens to him?"

Pam set Smokey down inside Cindy's apartment and nodded as she closed the door, not saying much more to her. Pam just wanted Smokey safe, and now he was. *Now let Larry try something.* "I'm going to make sure that you don't do anything to Smokey," she declared.

Larry had been here before. People always thought it was his doing; that somehow he was killing. How could they think that, and why? It was as if they could not believe it; they could not understand it. So it just had to be him, because that was the only thought they could get their minds around. How could Pam think this about him? He was now stressed and pulled out the stone and keychain in his pocket. He started to play with it. Pam was walking back towards him. He needed to confront her about this. But forcing Pam to understand what was going on inside his head had never been easy.

"Pam, I wouldn't hurt Smokey. Why would you say such a thing?" he said, defensively.

Pam was almost apt to believe him. Sure, Larry was strange. But could he really hurt others? Would he really kill Smokey? But, then again, there was that cop who stopped by the other day to question Larry. And what about the old lady on the street? Or Frank? And what about the way the hypnotist and the shaman had reacted to him? Perhaps she had better play it safe with Smokey. Just in case.

"Well, just make sure," she said aloud. "That cop stopped by the other day. He thought you were somehow linked to some deaths, and wanted my own views on it."

For the first time, Larry hated that he told her. He should not have let her win. Why did he open up to her? He knew better. He should have gone with what his gut said and kept his mouth shut. Now she might tell the cop, and that would be like giving a dog a bone; the cop would keep working it until he made something out of it. Police live for clear hard facts, until they could make them add up. And Larry was sure that this particular cop wouldn't stop until he had put the pieces together.

"Pam! You can't tell him what I just said. They…"

Before he could complete his plea, Pam cut him off, and finished his sentence with,

"…will lock you up! Maybe that would be best for all. Then you can't get close to Smokey or others."

She did not really mean what she said, but she had to keep him on his toes, keep him guessing. Besides, it was always fun to play with him like that; he was so easy to unsettle. She felt that it was what kept their love life alive. Or, at least half-alive.

Now Larry was really scared. He shouldn't have told her. Maybe he could just say he had no idea what she was talking about, if she did tell the cop. Right! He would just say he had no idea. But he first needed to try to stop her from telling the cop, or anyone else.

"What are you saying, Pam? You know I love that cat. I'm not a killer. I just knew all those people were going to die. And that damn cop, he just kept giving me that look—like I did it. Then he was asking me questions…but asking you is another thing altogether. What else did he say?"

Pam was shocked at how assertive Larry was being. She had not seen this side of him much. She rather liked it, from time to time. It was nice when he gave her a little of a fight. But today she did not have time to really mess with him. She decided to set his mind at ease about the cop's queries.

"Say? Nothing. Well, he did say some killers have a split personality, a dark side that they hide from themselves. Sometimes they might not even know that they are the ones doing the killing. It's like they have a split self. They truly believe they have no involvement. They have no idea."

This did nothing to ease Larry's fears. He was still mad that he had told her about his secret. Now, she was going to use his admission against him. She would beat him over the head with it until he ended up in jail, or worse.

"This is unreal! I tell you my deepest, darkest secret, and you turn it back on me!"

Pam realized she needed to cool him down. "Hey, I'm just telling what I was told." She moved closer and lightly held his arm. It was the first semi-loving touch she had given him in a long time. Her voice softened. "Thanks for telling me. You're just messed up, not a killer. Come on, after all that, you're taking me out to dinner. No more about this. I'm not cooking tonight just so you can fall asleep again and I have to eat by myself..."

It was still important to get the message across to Pam, not to tell. "I've only told two other people, and both acted like you did at first. It's only a matter of time before you ask the big question."

But Pam had had her fill of asking questions. And she had way too many answers to process for one night. She was ready for their relationship to return to her asking questions and him refusing to answer. Their conversation had worn her out, and she wanted to get out of the apartment. Without answering him, she grabbed her bag, pulled Larry behind her, and headed out the door. She had enough of weirdness for one night. It was time to go eat.

Pam had moved on, Larry could see, and he was happy to go out and eat. As they walked past the door of the neighbor's apartment, he said, under his breath so Pam could not hear, "I'll miss you Smokey. You have been a great cat. Sorry I can't say goodbye."

He would miss that cat. True, he had not liked him at first. And true, Smokey never really cared for Larry. But they kind of grew on each other, the way he and Pam had. Smokey was a companion to spend the night with on the front room couch when Pam was in one of her moods, a pal to watch TV with. The thought of his death made Larry sad. Larry knew the people or pets in his life that would soon be gone, but how do you say goodbye? People who know they are dying of cancer sometimes lash out at the ones they love most because of envy at others around them, the "why me" feeling. Because of this, Larry had decided never to tell people when they were about to die. That also meant that he could never say goodbye properly. He just had to act like all was well in the world. He hated that; he really did. And he knew Smokey's time was coming soon. Yes, he would miss him. Goodbye, Smokey.

It was quiet on the walk to the café. Pam and Larry did not speak much; Larry didn't want to share any more with Pam. He had told her too much already, given her too much ammo to use against him should something go wrong. She liked always having something on him, to keep him under control. As for his job, this was a small town with no other suitable companies to apply to, so he was stuck, and they know it. He worked long hours so his boss would get bigger bonuses, but not him.

Larry liked the cozy café they headed to because he could sit outside at a table and watch people walk by. And if someone had the smell on him, he couldn't tell because the tables outside sat away from the sidewalk. Pam liked it too. There was often new food on the menu. Pam knew that Larry liked it; not sure why, but no matter. She planned to blow her diet tonight because she had earned it, dealing with Larry and what she had learned. She was going to go all out.

As they got comfortable in their seats and stated looking over the menu, Pam's phone rang; it was Cindy. She glanced up at Larry, but he was just looking down at his placemat, obviously not wanting to make eye contact with her. Cindy said Smokey had gotten out somehow. He had been hit by a car. He was gone. Larry could hear Cindy sobbing on the other end of the phone, repeating how sorry she was. "Are you sure?" Pam asked.

She certainly believed Cindy—why would she lie about this? But Pam was less certain about Larry. Did she really want to believe that Larry had been right? How could this be? Instead of crying, Pam softly said goodbye and hung up. She didn't have to tell Larry what had happened. She could see by his face that he already knew; he knew it before it happened.

Larry knew Smokey was gone. Now he could show that he missed him. Until now, he had to keep it inside, grieve alone. Now he could let the pain out. Pam's mouth hung open in her blank face. She is in shock, he realized. *Wait for it... Here it comes...*

Pam recovered a little. "OK bud, but what...why didn't you tell me? What the hell?"

Larry knew how it felt, like every gear in your brain had slipped; you couldn't grab hold of your thoughts. Your mind screams, "This can't be happening!" But this was not the big question. Sooner or later she would ask the big question, the question people ask when they fully realize that we all die.

So he beat her to it. "Next you'll ask me *how*. The answer is, I don't know. I don't know how it happens. I just know I can smell it.

"Then you'll ask me if any of our family or friends will die soon. That's the big question."

Pam said nothing for a time. Larry waited for the gears to reengage.

At last she spoke, but all she said was "well…"

Larry knew she wanted to know. Thankfully, the answer was no.

Pam asked more questions. Could he smell it over the phone? Could he stop it from happening? Was it always accurate? Why were there two smells? Did she smell?

Larry tried to answer as tactfully as possible. He didn't want to overload her with too much information. She seemed to calm down a little when he told her that she didn't have a death smell on her.

They got up and walked out of the café without ordering. It wasn't until they got home that she realized that they hadn't eaten, but that wasn't important. She had so many more questions for him, and one big thing to tell him.

They sat on the front room couch, and Larry offered an explanation. "My uncle was overweight and close to a heart attack from overeating. In the morning, he didn't smell of death. But by the end of a day of overeating, drinking, and smoking, the smell of death on him got stronger. With some people, it's their lifestyle that pushes them faster toward the end. Sometimes we can slow it down or even speed it up, by adjusting our habits. But then, sometimes it's just going to happen, like it did with

Smokey. You can't slow it down or speed it up."

Apparently this was a gift Larry had, Pam thought. If you could call it that. A gift that he didn't know how to use. A gift going to waste because he kept it to himself. But how do you use it? She didn't have any suggestions at the moment.

Pam and Larry walked back towards the bedroom. Abruptly, Pam stopped. "I think it's best if you sleep on the couch tonight. I need some alone time, some non-freak time. Call it whatever the hell you want, but I need to think this out. And you need to call Cindy."

Larry agreed to sleep on the couch, but tonight he would not be sharing it with Smokey. He was so alone. He had revealed his secret to Pam, thinking that would help, but he still felt alone. He grabbed the blanket off the back of the couch and glanced at the clock. It was too late now to call Cindy.

He laid down on his back, looking up at the ceiling. Larry could hear Pam moving around on the bed, tossing and turning. No doubt she was still upset over the loss of her cat, and, you might say, the loss of her peace. Likely she was still confused about what Larry had said, convinced he would know if she was going to die, if she died before him. He knew she wanted to make sense of it, make her world go back to the way it was before she knew about Larry and his secret, back where things added up and things seemed normal.

He saw Pam's shape outlined in the moonlight, coming out of the bedroom. He could see her body through the light top she had on, walking his way silently. That was odd; usually she would be announcing to the world that Pam was now entering the room. Things had changed. They would never be the same. This was not her style at all.

Pam was tired, but couldn't sleep. For once, she really needed to be in Larry's arms. Her cat could not provide comfort now; it was Larry she needed. She had not felt like that for a long time. With all that was going on, she had forgotten to tell him the big news, but it could wait. As she joined Larry on the couch, she leaned over and whispered in his ear. "I changed my mind. I don't want to know. I don't want to know when I'm going to die. Don't push me away if you know when I'm going to die, please don't do that."

Before Larry could respond, she wrapped herself around him and immediately fell asleep in his arms. Larry never got a chance to speak. He was surprised that she now wanted to be close to him. It was a new feeling, but a welcome one.

Contented, he drifted off to sleep.

Chapter Twelve
She Met With Death Happily

The next morning arrived too soon for Larry. He woke up remembering that he had fallen asleep on the couch. The night came back to him in parts. His body was screaming at him: don't forget about me. I'm in pain here, and there is someone on top of us! Larry wanted to shift Pam's weight. But at the same time, he wasn't sure if or when he would wake up so close to her again, so he just kept still. His flesh complained about Pam's extra weight pushing on joints and bones. She was not a heavy person, but even when it was only the cat sleeping on his chest, it got really uncomfortable after an hour or two.

The cat… Yes, the cat was gone. What a night! It was one of those nights when your life turned suddenly and went a different way, never to be the same again. Larry knew he could not

go back to who he was before it happened.
Neither could Pam. Something like that changed
your life forever.

Pam was starting to wake up. She was
looking around for something. *Probably
Smokey*, Larry thought. Soon it would all come
back to her, what had happened the night before.
He could see it happening in her eyes now, and
she was almost to the part of how they got on
the couch.

She leaned over and said, "Thanks for
opening up to me last night, Larry. It means a
lot to me. I know I can't be easy to live with. I
know I'm a selfish person. But this time, I had
good reasons. I had to know what you were
holding back from me. It has always stood
between us. I needed to know because I found
out last week that I am pregnant! We're going
to have a baby, and I need things to be okay
with us before the baby comes."

Shocked, Larry slowly absorbed this news. A baby! His baby? He was going to be a father? What? How?

Pam nodded and smiled. All those questions had one answer, "yes..."

She moved away and headed for the bathroom. "Yes, I'm pregnant with your child. Speaking of which, I need to pee for the two of us. Don't go anywhere." Pam closed the bathroom door. Soon he would be asking more questions, she thought, it is his turn to question now, to be confused. Last night it was her turn, now it was his.

But Larry was thinking that he and Pam should start anew today. A fresh start. They both had questions. But maybe today wasn't the day for them. Maybe they should just enjoy their time together.

Larry could see a candle sitting on the end table. He had never noticed it before. The design was quite unusual. There was a white pillar candle in the center, while intricately carved people were standing around it, holding hands. It seemed to have some kind of meaning, but he wasn't sure what. "Pam," he called, "Is this a new candle? What's with all the people standing around it?"

Pam had forgotten that she had bought the candle for Larry. "Oh, yeah," she called back from the bathroom. "It's a talisman. I picked it up the other day. It's for Day of the Dead. The salesman said it's a Latin holiday. Something about honoring dead loved ones. I think it's today."

Larry's dad and mom were dead, but he decided to put the candle to good use. Maybe they could use the candle to share their good news with his parents.

"You're supposed to light the candle and put it by a private altar honoring the deceased. You can use the favorite foods and beverages of the departed or some special symbol representing them."

It would be easy for them to find something from his mother, but Larry had no idea what his dad liked or disliked. He had never known his father. And his mother had hated talking about him. Larry guessed that it pained her that he had left without a word—no explanation, no I'm sorry, no nothing. So Larry never asked too many questions, not wanting to hurt his mother.

In fact, Larry was unsure whether his father was alive or dead. He had read a story once, about a mother who skipped out and never came back. No one knew why. Twenty years later, as the city prepared to build a new bridge over the river, construction workers found a car under the water. The woman was in it. She had apparently slipped off the road and drowned. Twenty years ago. Larry wanted to think that something like that had happened to his father. That he hadn't just ran out.

Larry took the birthstone keychain from his pocket and placed it next to the candle. He struck a match and set the candle aglow. "Well, all dead family and friends," he announced awkwardly, "I'm going to be a dad." For the first time in months, Larry let out a genuine smile. He was going to be a dad. There was nothing better in the world. He was going to be a dad!

Larry let the candle's smoke dance around the room before sitting back down on the couch. But then he noticed a man standing in the corner of the room, in the shadows. Larry froze. The man moved towards him, faster and faster until he stood in front of Larry. *What the—*

"Congrats on having a baby," the man started. "It's going to be a boy."

Larry looked around the room for something that he could use as a weapon, if need be. Next to the couch, he noticed the stick they used to prop open the windows. He grabbed it and made himself ready. "Who the hell are you? How did you get in here? What do you want?"

The bathroom door opened, and Pam walked out, a towel wrapped around her. Larry placed himself between the stranger and Pam, facing the man to make sure he didn't take one step toward his wife. Larry had always considered himself a bit of a wimp, but now it was time to stand up for his wife and his unborn child.

Pam looked at Larry like he was crazy. He was standing there as if he was guarding her from something. She shook her head and passed him by on her way to the kitchen. She retrieved a bar of soap from one of the grocery bags and returned to the living room. Larry was still standing there, half crouched and ready to pounce. The stick was slung around one shoulder as if he was playing baseball. Or, getting ready to attack someone. But who? Her?

"Did I scare you?" She peered at him. "Larry, you look scared to death. Why are you holding that stick? You know, you really need to stop this crazy stuff." Pam went back into the bathroom and turned the water off. "Larry," she called, "I'm going to take a bath—I mean, a shower."

Larry couldn't believe how nonchalant Pam was acting. Obviously she hadn't seen the stranger in the corner, or she would have freaked out. He mumbled, "Bath…shower…what?"

"You're not supposed to take hot baths when you're pregnant. The baby can't cool down when it's surrounded by hot water," she answered. She closed the bathroom door, leaving Larry and the stranger alone.

"She can't see you," he said, puzzled.

"No," the stranger replied. "Only you can see me."

"What? Why? What the hell is going on here? Who are you? What are you doing here?" Apparently, this was going to be another question filled day.

"Only a handful of us are given the gift, if you want to call it that," said the stranger. "Some people call it a gift. I call it a job."

Larry's body suddenly seemed massive. His knees wanted to bend and put him on the floor in a quivering mass of fear. He felt like he was going to pass out. The stress—he'd been through too much recently, no wonder he felt dizzy. He gathered himself together with effort. "What gift—or job—is that?" he asked, trying to keep the fear out of his voice. "What are you talking about?"

The stranger stepped closer and placed his hand on Larry's shoulder. Frozen with fear, Larry could not move away. He had an odd feeling inside. Something had changed; it was weird. He looked at the spot on his shoulder were the man had touched him, but nothing was there to give him any kind of a clue.

The man stepped back. "Larry, the ability to see things that most do not see, to smell things others can't smell, that's your gift."

Though others had called it a "gift," Larry didn't consider these things any kind of a gift. It was more of an annoyance, or had been so far. And how did this guy, whoever he was, know about it?

Again the bathroom door opened and out stepped Pam, with her towel. She had forgotten her razor and needed to get it before taking a shower. She called for Larry. When he didn't answer, she decided he must have gone out for something.

In fact, Larry had answered Pam when she first came into the room, but she had ignored him. He moved around in front of her, but it soon became obvious that she couldn't see *him* either. "Now she can't see *me*," he complained.

The stranger chuckled. "No, and you don't want her to, not yet. I'm glad you told her last night about your gift."

This is tiring, Larry thought. He was asking questions, but not getting any answers, much less the right ones. "How did you know I have this gift?" he demanded. "Who the hell are you, and what the hell is going on?"

The stranger sat down in the nearest chair. "Let's just say I'm 'family.' And on this holiday, I'm starting you in the family business. Kind of like your own franchise. Best part is, no franchise fees. And it's all but impossible for you to fail."

Just when Larry thought he couldn't be any more confused, he was. "Next you'll say I'm going to be rich and have a ton of money."

The dark man paused, and then went on. "Wealthy? Yes, in one way. But you'll make no money to speak of. Sit down, and I'll tell you about it."

Larry sat as directed. He didn't know if he had done so out of curiosity or terror.

"I can answer many of your questions, maybe most of them. So ask away."

"All right. Once again, who or what the hell are you?"

"What am I? Good question. When Eve picked the fruit from the Tree of Knowledge, she knew that meant that she was mortal: in time, she would die. She started the family line and created the demand for us. From that point on, one of her offspring would always carry the calling. That child was the start of our family line."

"Are you the devil?"

"No, I'm the rot on the apple after it's been sitting on your desk too long. I'm the dark shadow that you see when you turn your head too fast. I'm the shape at the end of the hall you can't quite make out. I'm the thing in the room when your brain tells you you're alone but your stomach is tells you you're not. I hide in your blind spot, but you can feel me there."

This was starting to smell of BS to Larry. It looked to him like this person had broken in and was now trying to get out of it. But still, Pam not seen the stranger, and now she couldn't see Larry, either. Maybe he was dead. No, that couldn't be right; his heart was alive and racing. "What kind of crap is this? This wasn't in any textbook I ever read."

"I'm tired of this 'What, what, what.' I'm tired of that word," growled the stranger.

This kind of pissed Larry off; he knew he sounded like Pam, but he had to know.

"Okay, new word, 'who.' As in, *who* the hell are you?"

The stranger didn't answer right away. Eventually he started. "In Zoroastrianism, I'm Mayra. In Babylon, I am Mot. The Arabic is Azrael. In Muslim and Islam theology, I'm Azrael who is 'forever writing in a large book and forever erasing what he writes.' In Judeo-Christian, I'm the angel of death. To Hollywood, I'm the grim reaper."

Larry drew in his breath. This was some heavy stuff, a lot take in. "You're Death? You're here for me? Already?"

Death knew he had taken a toll on poor Larry today. "Again, yes and no. Yes, I am Death. And yes, I am here for you. But no, you're not dying. I'm here for a different reason."

Larry sat up. Pam had really struggled trying to believe he could smell death. Now he understood why. This *entity* was asking him to believe that he was Death, but Larry couldn't wrap his head around it. "You don't look like Death, but…I suppose…"

Death chuckled. "How about this?" He turned around once. When he faced Larry again, he looked just like the man Larry had seen in the street the day that the old lady had taken ill.

"Each person sees me differently, you know." Death turned around again, and he was a young boy. "To the young, I might look like any other child taking them off to play."

Another turn and Death changed again, this time appearing a black-robed skeleton wielding a scythe. "It was some artist in the 15th century that made the Grim Reaper take on the dark, hooded robe persona," said Death. "The image evolved from the traditional garb of pallbearers at funerals—the dark robe with a bowed head. Artists took the image to a more horrific level by making the person under the robe either a rotting corpse, a skeleton, or just complete blackness. They weren't aware that they had the power to see us."

Death turned a final time and shifted back to his "normal" appearance.

"But if you're Death," Larry mused, "why can't I smell you? I can smell when someone is dying a mile away. Why can't I smell Death himself when he's sitting in my living room?"

Death chuckled. "The smell *calls* us; it's not *part* of us. We are more like bees attracted to the smell of a flower. It's the smell of a person approaching his or her time. Some people can smell it. Some people can even see us. Soldiers on the battlefield, the elderly in nursing homes, sick people in hospitals, and people from all walks of life have reported seeing a dark, shadowy figure that they don't believe is human. When their minds are busy with the emotions that come with realizing they're going to die, they no longer block out things."

Larry sat there, stunned and speechless.

Death hurried to pick up the dead air. He seldom got to talk, and when he did, it was only a few words to someone before they went into the light. So he enjoyed talking to Larry. He had waited for this day for a long time and still had much to tell him. "The other day, you saw Death on the sidewalk. Now it's your time to join us."

Larry said nothing.

"We get a bad rap, you know." Death yawned, then went on. "It's the nature of this job. I'm perceived as dark and evil. The reality is, although death often seems unfair, we are neither good nor evil. You could say we're the true middle men. Death: it's simply a fact of life, like the sun rising in the morning. The sun isn't good or evil; it provides warmth, light, and energy for plants to grow. But, if you were starving because of a drought, or stuck in a desert with no water, the sun is definitely not your friend. The sun is indifferent.

"Perspective is everything. People see me as they can, or want to, or are able to, whatever their minds can handle. Many find it difficult to cope with death. It's the great equalizer, the unknown, the one place people are trapped. Once there, they can't come back. Some see death as a dark game. They're always trying to beat me, or cheat me, or bargain their way out of it."

"A game, what game?"

Death shrugged. "A game you cheat at, as they have with so many of the games they played in life. Most people spend so much time trying to get ahead that they can't enjoy their life. Only at the end of their days do they understand. At the end, it all goes back in each person's box, and only Death gets to play again. Some people are really into the subject because it's the one big thing mankind has not been able to overcome."

Larry had been slouching, but now he sat up straight. "I understand, I think. But what does this have to do with me? You didn't come here to collect me or remove my name from the great book, did you?" He assumed that, if Death wanted to take him, he already would have.

Death leaned forward and locked eyes with Larry. They were dark and compelling. Larry wanted to scratch his nose, but he couldn't move his arm. He couldn't move anything.

"Larry, listen to me. Do you ever wonder why you haven't many friends? Why people don't spend more time with you? Why they act like they're scared of you? You must have wondered why they don't want to get to close to you, why they're not sure if they can trust you. You were told it was your low self-esteem—not having a father around as you grew, spending too much time by yourself, and so on. But that's not it. Can't you feel someone's life force when you're close to them, the strength of their life? It jumps at you like a loud television ad. When you're next to a child with years of life ahead, you probably feel like you're floating next to the sun. But when you're next to someone almost at the end of their life, you feel as cold as the longest day of winter."

Larry felt relieved to hear this. He had never put it into words before, or had it put into words for him. It was so weird, having someone understand it the way he did. This might not actually be Death, but whomever or whatever he was, he did understand. And Larry was grateful for that. Larry wasn't sure where Death was going with all of this talk, but he did feel a little more comfortable. "Yeah," he mumbled, "I guess, now that you say that, yes..."

Death could feel Larry coming around. Now it was time to set the hook. "How about the smell, like the smell of an apple that has been set out too long and has gone bad, telling the insects, 'It's time to come and get it.' The bugs are like the cleanup crew. Larry, the universe is built to clean up after itself, and we are the cleanup crew." Death could see and feel that Larry was still unsatisfied, that he still wanted to know what this had to do with him. Unfortunately, many of life's mysteries—or, in this case, Death's mysteries—can't be answered so easily.

"You know," said Death, "I was once married to a lovely woman. I really cared for her, as you care for your wife, though we had our ups and downs. But then one day a man came to me, as I have come to you. He was my father. I had just found out my wife was pregnant. After my talk with my dad, I never got to spend time with my wife again, until she died. I never got to hold my son, see him born, or go to a game with him. In fact, I never got to talk to my son, until today."

Larry couldn't believe what he was hearing. He just sat there, not moving. It felt like Death had pulled the life force out completely of his body, but he could not believe that either.

Death smiled to himself. He could almost hear the gears in Larry's brain jumping and skipping as they stripped parts off what he had heard. He looked like a clock that someone had wound too tightly until the gears stripped. Death was waiting for it all to soak in. It was a big idea. Death knew that Larry only thought about himself and how he was different, that he had gone through his whole life wondering why he was strange. Sometimes, the answer isn't what we want to hear.

Was Death was trying to tell him that he, Larry, was Death's son?

Death tried again, "Larry, listen close. The same way I come to you today, my father came to me. My biggest regret in life was that I never got to talk to my son—*you*—until today."

Larry bent down in the chair and put his head in his hands.

"That's right, you're my son."

Larry shook his head. So much weight in his brain, it was exhausting. He had dreams of meeting his dad one day, but he never expected *this.* He had laughed at lighting the candle, yet somehow it had worked. Larry didn't feel as if he knew enough to decide whether what the stranger said was true or not. *My father is the angel of death? Does this make me more weird, or less weird. Maybe he's delusional—my father's a freak! He makes me look normal!* He called out to Pam and tell her, "Hey, honey! If you think I'm a freak, meet my dad. It's in my genes. I have freaked-out designer genes." He started laughing maniacally.

Death knew that Larry was close to going over the edge. He needed to calm down. "Larry, Pam can't hear you now."

Larry cut him off; this was too much, and the only way he could handle it was to somehow laugh it off, or lose it. He chose to laugh. "Oh! Pam," he said loudly, "would you like to meet my dad? He's the angel of death. Just don't look into his eyes or you'll die…"

"You can't talk to Pam right now, Larry."

"Okay," Larry continued jovially, "but this will be great at family get-togethers. You want to meet my dad? Boom! And the guy falls dead after seeing you. Or better yet, hey, heavy metal bands, you're singing about my dad! You want to meet him? Oh, that's right, many of you already have." Larry laughed nervously. "What the hell? Meet my dad, he is a dead ringer for the Grim Reaper, I bet people are dropping dead to meet you, Dad. Hah! Hah!"

Death didn't have any experience at keeping Larry under control, but he had to get some, fast. "It's good to see you can joke about this, son."

"*Joke about it*? I'm not joking. Can't you see I'm losing it?"

Death spoke sharply: "So, I've waited years to talk to you, and this is what you have to say?"

Larry could tell Death did not know much about fathering. He'd not had a very good role model, either.

"All right," said Death, trying to change the subject. "Tell me what you do for a living." Of course, from now on Larry would spend his time walking the earth plucking souls from bodies, but he'd save that for later.

Larry grunted. "I'm in IT. I work for a company called Picket."

"Did you say 'Picket'?"

"Yeah. The owner hit it big by creating a website showing people picking their noses, and it just took off. I update the site and keep it going."

As he went around collecting souls, Death had watched the internet come on, larger and stronger every day. He didn't really need to know more, but if there was ever a time for pretending, this was it. "So you spend time with a website that shows people picking their noses. And you think being Death is weird?"

"Listen, Death, or whoever you are. So my job is nothing to die for, or not to die for, as the case may be, but what about my family, my friends? What about them?"

Death shrugged. "They will not know us but once."

"What's this 'us' business?"

"I'm talking about you and me, son. And our forefathers, our ancestors, the other Grim

Reapers. We go back many generations, of course. We each take care of an assigned part of the world. We all wait for the Eschatology, the 'end-of-time,' the day we are all called out of retirement to clean up the mess humans have made of the world."

Larry's breath caught in his throat as he realized, for the first time, what he was really being asked to do. This was not some light thing. This was big, the biggest thing in the world after, maybe, being born. He didn't think it would be much fun doing it. What would he say when people asked him what he did for a living? I kill people?

"What do you mean, 'cleanup'?" he asked instead.

"Larry, the human race is in a giant game of tug-of-war with utter destruction. Some days, the humans win; other days, destruction wins. In the end, the humans will certainly lose. Then we will be called to collect all the remaining souls. 'Cleanup.' Yes, you will a soul collector. You can never again be close to anybody. If Pam could see you now, she would die. You're now part of us now. Part of the family. When I touched your shoulder, you became Death. Like me. You can't write her, either, for yours is the hand of Death. If she were to read a letter written by you, she would die. You must keep her alive so your son will someday be able to join the family business. From now on, you will no longer be a passenger in your own life, but the pilot."

Larry said nothing. He couldn't believe he wasn't part of Pam's world any more. This had really hit home for him, and it was almost too much to understand. "Last year I took a DNA test," he said slowly, looking at the carpet, "They said it would tell me about my father's ancestry, about his blood line. But it came back, 'unconfirmed.'"

Death nodded. "You wouldn't have any luck with that, son. Our DNA would not be on file."

"But...how did all this start? How did it happen? It's just too weird. Where did I come from if you are my father? *Who am I?*"

"Blood line? What blood line? Your blood line is Death! As to how it happened, one of our ancestors won a favor with the current powers that be. Call it 'God' if you want. He was given one wish. He asked for all his descendants to live long and never die, not growing old like everyone else did. He got his wish, and all his descendants became Reapers. He didn't realize that the world runs by the Laws of Movement. Time is movement; movement is change; change is movement, and so on.

"A decision became necessary: we could change all the laws of movement, space, and time, or connect with and obey the laws already in place. It's a law: people must die. So he became Death. Death's mission was, and is, to walk the earth until the end of time. It may not have been the best choice, but he chose it out of love, trying to do the best for us all. The story is told over and over, in all cultures: someone wants immortality so desperately that they are willing to do whatever it takes to get it, and it ends by blowing up in their face."

For the first time, Death's eyes revealed a little emotion: sadness. Larry hadn't seen any emotion before in Death's eyes. They were pretty much as he imagined they would be: empty, blank, and emotionless. If this stranger was really Death, he must have seen plenty of sadness in others. He must have grown used to it long since. Maybe it was the pain of revealing all this to his son that made his eyes fill with sorrow.

Larry felt bad for Death, but still, he didn't want any of this; it wasn't the life he had chosen. Everybody else had choices, and the freedom to choose. He ought to have been able to choose some other life, but he feared there was no way out of it.

All of a sudden, Larry remembered reading once that wealthy Romans would pay someone to fill in for them in the army. The stand-ins would serve in the military for money. Maybe Death would accept some such arrangement. *Wouldn't hurt to ask.* "A lot of people would probably love to do this. I saw some kids the other day running around in black clothing, painting their faces white, looking like death warmed over…oh, sorry, no offense. They poke holes in every part of their bodies—the Goth look, they call it. Why not pick one of them? You could adopt one of them and disown me. It doesn't *have* to be me, does it?"

It was hard being Death; it was even harder trying to get someone else to do it, and your son on top of that. True, the job was not one most would pick, but it did have its benefits, like living until the end of time. But persuading your son to take it over was definitely a downer. Larry's response was completely natural: "why me"? The logical answer was "Why not you? Why should you not be the one to stand up and do it?" This feeble answer did not sit well with Larry.

Death could see that Larry was looking for a way out of the situation. There was one way, but Death hated having to tell him. It was not good. Larry had been born to this job. It was his life's calling, the reason he was put on this earth. It called him, and he must respond.

Larry could see his dad was deep in thought. He didn't care; he just wanted to live. He might have a crappy life, but it was *his* life. He wanted, he wanted to live it, and without even thinking, he yelled it out: "I want to live!"

This was a cry Death had heard many times while taking people's souls. It was their last yell, their last hope. So he was not surprised to hear it coming from Larry. After all, he was asking Larry to end his life and take up a different one. He was asking him to walk away from everything he knew.

"You call this living?" Death asked, a bit harshly. "You just float through, day-to-day. You hate your job because you seem to be the only one that cares. Your bosses are only interested in short-term profit. They don't care about their employees. They just want to suck the company dry and jump ship. And, in the end, there you are, left with a sinking ship. But you can get out of that rat race. Now you can leave all that behind. A door has opened to you."

This just upset Larry more. Death made it sound like he was asking him to be Santa Claus or something. But this was being Death! What kind of business card would you get for that kind of work? So he wasn't a rock star—he had to sit in cubicle all day, that looked and felt like a jail cell, next to someone who reeked of smoke unless he was passing gas, which was often. But you could at least put your title on a business card. Better yet, you could talk to people about it with no danger to them. And that was it in a nutshell. Yes, he was alone; he did not have a lot of friends, but he could say hi to someone in the park or on the street, and they could smile back. After all those years of feeling alone, Larry realized he was a part of something. He was part of the human race. And now Death—his father—was asking him to give that up.

On top of that, Pam was pregnant. He was going to be someone's father. He couldn't think of anything better. He was really looking forward to that, but now his dad wanted to take that all away from him. His dad had stepped out of his childhood, and took part of it with him. Now he wanted Larry to pass it along to his own child. No, no, no! That was not going to happen!

Death could see that Larry was not far from understanding; he needed to try something else. "Now it's time to take your place in the family business, Larry. It's my gift to you, as it will be to your son."

Larry had been cooling off, but this kicked his anger up even higher. "My gift? I never got crap from you for years! You walked out, missed all my birthdays, school events, everything. How about the gift you gave me when mom died and I sat by myself at her funeral? No one next to me in church—how about that? Where were you then? And now that I have something great happening in my life, you pull this crap! Why don't you go away and leave me alone, so I can have my life. You messed me up as a child when you left, and now you've messed me up by coming back. So, just go."

Larry's dad felt his pain He wished he could just go, as Larry wished, but it was impossible. Maybe it was time for some kind words. "I'm trying to make this as positive as I can, Larry. It is a gift. Not exactly a blessing, but a family duty you are born into. I can't give back that time I missed, when I was called to do this and could not be with you. But I can now spend time with you and show you what to do. Teach you. You will have years of time to spend with me. I'll make it up. Again, I'm sorry."

But it didn't help. Larry remained furious. What did he know about being sorry? What a jerk. He remembered in grammar school, a teacher found Larry crying in the cloak room after a father and son event. All of the other boys had fathers or uncles show up. Larry had no one. Someone from the Big Bothers organization was supposed to come, but the guy canceled at the last minute. It was too late for Larry to back out, so he'd gone by himself. Other kids made fun of him. The teacher had tried to console him: "I know you're sad, and hurting, but my father never came to this event either; he was too busy getting drunk, or playing golf with his friends, or beating one of us. I can truly say, sometimes it's best to not have someone around. For years I prayed that he would just leave. And when he did, it was the best day of my life."

Larry hadn't understood that at the time, but he did now. He just wanted his dad to leave him alone. As a kid, he had it in his mind that his dad would someday come back, and they would spend time together, the way fathers and sons are supposed to. The kids who made fun of him at the father-son events would see him and be jealous of him, as he once was of them. But who would be jealous of this crap?

Why can't I just be normal? The thought that he might never again be normal made him even more resentful and sad. "Sorry?" he shouted. "Now you're sorry? Do you know what it was like, how it hurt watching other kids' dads hug them, waiting for that feeling—even for just a second? I was a good kid. Why, Dad? Why me? What could I have done to make me deserve that?"

Death could feel the hurt in Larry's voice. He had tried, but it was like waves hitting the hard shores of a rocky beach, words breaking up on Larry's mind and not going in. He couldn't be heard because Larry's defenses would not allow it. How do you overcome years of pain in a day, or an hour? How do you take the pain of a long separation, of being different, of being the outsider and, most of all, of feeling weird and alien in your world?"

Death sighed. "It was nothing you did, son, nothing at all. It was just…inevitable. A law of nature, you might say."

But Larry again blocked his words. There was just too much resistance inside him, pushing them back. Sadly enough, Death understood his long-lost son. Larry's life was also his life, at one time. But that didn't change anything; Larry must be made to understand their mission in life. Others were like crops planted on the face of the earth; someday they had to be harvested. But he and Larry were exceptions, not crops. They stood with the harvesters.

It felt stuffy in the apartment. It was time to get some fresh air, and get Larry in more of a neutral place. "Larry, let's go for a walk," his father suggested.

Larry agreed, and they went outside. As soon as the door closed behind them, he smelled something. It was that smell again, the one he knew all too well. It was coming from under the Cindy's door. She was so nice, and Larry really liked her. He didn't want her to die. Maybe it was the smell of Smokey's passing lingering in her apartment? He hoped that was it.

Death opened the Cindy's door and walked inside without even knocking. Not thinking, Larry walked in after him. Now that

Larry was inside, he could tell the smell was not from Smokey, but coming from Cindy. He wished he had spent more time with her now.

Cindy was sitting in her rocking chair, rocking back and forth. Death saw that this was Larry's first opportunity to do what he had been put on the earth to do. The first couple of attempts were always the hardest.

"Larry, you can smell it, can't you?" he asked, softly. "This is your first job. Everyone has their day. It's not for us to choose who goes. We just go where we are needed, when we are called. It's not easy, but you must do it."

Larry didn't think he could. Cindy was so nice; she had been so kind to him and Pam and Smokey. Why did it have to be her? And why did he have to do this? Maybe this was all a dream—a nightmare—maybe it was all an illusion, maybe he had lost it at last.

He closed and then opened his eyes, hoping it would all vanish, but it didn't. His dad looked the same. Cindy looked the same. He looked at Death, tears in his eyes. "Why her?" he choked. "She's so nice…"

Death laid a bony hand on his shoulder. "I can tell you, she will be thankful. You didn't know it, but she has been suffering for a long time. She feels the pain a child feels, who has been left behind and is waiting for her parents to come take her home."

Larry had never thought of it that way. Death made it sound as if what they were about to do was a good thing. But Larry also knew that it robbed people of love and put pain in its place.

Cindy could not see or hear them, though they were standing right next to her. "What about that tunnel stuff, the white light and all that?" he asked.

"Yes, the white light and the tunnel are there," Death replied, "but we can't go into the light. We simply split the body from the soul.

Sometimes the body jumps after the soul, sometimes not."

Larry shook his head. "But what's it like on the other side?"

For Death, this was a difficult question to answer. It was like trying to explain "blue" to someone who had never seen it. At best, Larry's dad only got a fast look at it, since it was on the other side. Like living creatures, Death was trapped in the middle world.

"From what I see, you get rewarded or punished for what you love in life," said Death. "On the other side, some pay for what they tried to hide in their life. We can get into this more later. Right now, it's time for you to call her home, regardless of what happens to her on the other side."

Larry just realized with all the questions and what was going on, that they had not gone outside for Fresh air as they had talked about. He now knew that his dad had a plan for him, and that he was carrying it out. Larry realized that he didn't have a choice in the matter. For the rest of their time on the planet, he and his dad would have to finish their jobs. No walks in the park. No drives down the shore. No bonding sessions at a baseball game. All business, all the time.

On the other hand, Larry always did like cleaning up after things. He tried to align his thinking with Death's explanation. Maybe this *was* just one big clean-up job. He was cleaning up the souls and sending them on their way. Pam had never let him clean. If he tried cleaning the kitchen, she would kick him out and come screaming in from the other room if he tried to load the dishwasher. If he did manage to load it, she would reload it, and start it immediately. Sometimes she even stood guard over him, making sure he stayed away from the kitchen.

He started remembering some of the other things about his life that had irritated him.

He hated having to worry if his clothing was in style, or his hair or his car. All that was over if he did this. He could be through trying to make other people happy. Larry was beginning to think rationally, and the idea of going with his father started to sound better. At least he'd be able to come and go as he pleased, no cares. No more feeling like he was a rat in a cage, just wanting to get out. He could be free now. If only it weren't for that one down side—having to take someone's life. But then again, wasn't he just helping them pass over into a new life? It was all in your perspective, like marketing. He still wondered, though, how would he feel doing this. Could he even do it? Would it hurt his victims, or himself?

It did help that for the first time in his life he felt he had a purpose, a mission. He also had the freedom to come as go as he wished. No more clock to watch at work, waiting for it to closing time so he could go. And wasn't his life at home just another jail? He spent most of his time sitting around waiting for Pam's approval. Killing time is what he really did most days. That and trying not to upset others. The only free time he had was to or from work. But now he could belong to something. He had always wanted to feel like he belonged. This new calling would be like being admitted to a selective country club. On top of that, he didn't have to change anything about himself or hide anything. He could fit in just by being himself.

He'd always felt out of place even in the weirdest of groups. He once belonged to a group of people who each had "some extra special unique talent." He had read about them in the newspaper. There was something weird or crazy about each of them. At their meetings, each would tell their story, which ranged from seeing colors around people, to hearing dead people talk, to his own ability to smell death. They all listened to the stories, but they kept their shock or disbelief to themselves. He had felt okay about himself in that group. He knew the others wouldn't judge him out loud (even if they were all judging one another in their heads). The group of Reapers, however, would be even better. He belonged automatically, without doing anything. He'd been born into it. He was beginning to understand and accept it, and maybe, just maybe, it was time for him to give it a try. But he still felt uncomfortable. He reached for his birthstone keychain, but it wasn't there. He had put it next to the candle and forgot to pick it up again.

"Okay, Dad. So if I was to do this, what would I do next?" He was hoping that he wouldn't have to hit her over the head, or strangle her with a phone cord, or push her down the stairs. If he had to go that far, then he would have to rethink this whole thing. In fact, if he had to do any of those things, maybe his dad wasn't who he said he was. Maybe the cop was right. But for now, he would play alone and see what was next.

Death softly grabbed Larry by the arm and led him over to the rocking chair. For some reason, Larry's dad started thinking about why old people like to sit and rock in chairs. They were in motion, but not going anywhere, not doing anything. Many people do this kind of busy work, killing time, just to have something to do, but never really getting anywhere. Life had so many possibilities, things you could do. He remembered once calling on a man who had been in an accident years earlier, which had cost him the use of his arms and legs. After being confined to his bed for a long time, the man started a company and ran it from his bed. There is so much people can do, Death reflected, but many too many people get stuck at the salad bar and never got to the entries.

It looked like Cindy was staring at some old photos on the wall as she rocked. One, he was sure, was her late husband. It was just another day for her, sitting in her apartment, hoping one of her kids would call or stop by. As one song goes, "living after the thrill of living is gone." No doubt, she missed her husband, even the things he did that at one time drove her nuts. Both Larry and his father were surprised when she spoke aloud.

"I miss you, Albert," she murmured. "It's been some time now since you passed. I do hope there is an afterlife and we can be together again someday. I have so much I want to tell you, things that only you can understand. Things that only someone who spent a lifetime with you can comprehend. I miss you, and so many we used to know are also gone. I've outlived them all, and those who are still alive are too busy with their lives to bother with an old lady like me. I just have my memories now, my personal photo album in my head and heart. And that's fading with time and age."

Larry and his dad stood beside her. Larry's dad told him to touch Cindy's shoulder. Larry was scared. He didn't want to hurt her.

But he slowly reached out and lightly touched her shoulder. Slowly, she stood up, or her soul stood—her body stayed lifeless in the chair. She looked straight at Larry. She could see him now. To Larry, it appeared as if there were two of her, one lying in the chair, eyes closed dead to the world, and one standing right there in front of him, shining full of life. The smell was also gone now. The room smelled fresh and clean. Out of the corner of his eye, Larry saw a light. It was bright, and grew more intense by the second. It seemed to be some kind of doorway, with shinning gold as the door frame. But it was too bright to look at directly, so Larry couldn't make heads or tails out of it.

As Larry was tying trying to figure out the doorway, Cindy touched his arm. But it did not feel like a physical touch, more like a stir of the soul. With her touch, his eyes were back on her, not the doorway. He could see that Cindy was happy to see him. "Larry? What are you doing here? How did you get in? Who is that with you? You scared me to death!"

Larry didn't reply. He sensed that he needed to move fast, that time was key here. He needed to get her moving before she asked too many questions.

Death spoke before Larry had time to. "I'm Larry's father, and your wait is over. Your family and friends are waiting for you." He pointed at her body, still sitting in the chair. Cindy looked at herself, then at the light coming from the door. She looked into the light. Larry tried looking as well, but he could see only vague shapes. He couldn't make out faces or anything like that, just shapes of light. It was breathtaking to say the least.

Cindy walked toward the light, joy written all over her. "Albert? Is that you?" she cried, rushing forward. Larry heard something, but couldn't quite make it out what was being said back to her. Maybe because it was not meant for him. The nice lady next door, that he knew and loved, stepped into the light and was gone as the light faded. Soon it was completely gone, leaving an empty spot in his heart as if he had missed out on something great. The only thing left was a sweet smell that lightly filled the room. The smell was also going fast. He hadn't noticed it before, as he was in awe of the doorway, but it had also come at the same time. The smell was more like roses than anything else. But now that the door was gone, the more he tried to smell the wonderful aroma, the more it died down.

Larry felt sad that he hadn't say goodbye to Cindy. It had all happened so quickly that he forgot. He had just experienced one of the biggest mysteries in the history of mankind: what happens to us when we die? He was speechless, but still he regretted not spending more time with Cindy when he had the chance. The list of regrets went on and on, things he should have done but hadn't. He was sure her kids would have the same feeling now that she was gone.

Some would say Cindy had led a very simple life, others that her life had been hard. She had lived through the dirty 30s, when the family lost the farm after her father died. She had lived long; she had seen and done many things, but now it was all gone. Her family could not ask any more questions about family history, spend a day with her, or tell her how much they loved her. It was done.

Larry could not help staring at her body, just lying in the chair like a coat someone had taken off and left behind. It was over; the hard part of her life was over. Her family would mourn. A gathering had greeted her on the other side: her friends, her sister and bothers who had beaten her to the light, meant that only a few remained to show up for her funeral. Her kids would be there, and some of her grandkids who would only remember her as someone who could not afford to spend much on them for Christmas.

Somehow, Larry knew all this. He had watched her walk into the light, and now he saw her life flash in front of him. He knew her thoughts and the thoughts and feelings of her loved ones. He thought he was wise before, believed he knew so much, but he really knew nothing. Only now did he understand that the people we come in contact with are really walking books of information, just wanting to be read, if we would only take the time. We are in the habit of looking to the web or the TV for answers, but people are the great information base. The less we have in common with someone, he thought, the more we can learn from them. Someone once told him, "water is the last thing a fish understands as it jumps out and dies on the land." He figured that was what life was like for people—life was the last thing they really understood until they died. Hard to understand something you're in the middle of.

Larry noted how empty Cindy's body looked. Larry had seen a couple of dead people before and noticed that they looked like they should sit up and talk. But now that he had seen Cindy's soul leave her body, he realized that the corpse was only a vessel.

Cindy's cat now entwined itself around her legs, purring and nuzzling against her, as if she could reanimate her owner. Larry could feel the cat's pain, the loss. He said the first thing that came to mind: "Toto, I've got a feeling she not in Kansas anymore."

Overall, it had not been so hard. Larry turned to his father. "Is that it? Just like that? It's done?"

Larry's dad expected it to be hard for Larry; he'd known her, after all. Still, it hadn't been that complicated. The next one would be much harder to collect. Cindy had had a good life. She met with death happily. She was a good person and hers was a good ending. Of course, having a good life didn't guarantee an easy death, only an easy transition to the next life. But this was something Larry would have to learn the hard way.

Chapter Thirteen
The Shaman's Time

"Larry, it's time to get some fresh air now. Let's go outside."

As they walked out of the apartment building, Larry quietly thought to himself. He had many questions jumping around in his brain, but how do you start and where? It was difficult to absorb everything he had just experienced. Most people saw this event happen once in a lifetime—at their own death. They weren't left behind to ponder what they had seen. They would not be able to talk about it with anybody still here on earth. But for him, he would have to witness this day after day after day. He was not sure he was ready for this, not sure if he could do it.

The glow and newness was starting to wear off. And what about Cindy's family? What could be done for them? He remembered

how much he missed his mom when she died.
Yes, he hadn't see her all that often in her later
years, but, once she was gone, he missed her.
Now she'd never know he was going to be a
father. With that thought, Larry's anger came
raging back; the feeling of peace was gone. He
wanted to be a father! The whole show he'd
imagined after Pam told him was fading away,
and his anger was coming back. It was directed
at his dad. His dad was a killer.

"So Dad, who is your boss? Who do you
report to? I want to talk to them. When is the
next team meeting?"

Death believed that anybody that started
a questions with the word "so" was really asking
a different question. For example, the real
question behind "So, what's for dinner
tonight?"was "Is it something I like or not? If
it's not, I'm eating a snack now." What Larry
was wanting to know, probably, was his boss's

name and location, so he could argue his way of out the job with the person in charge.

Death laugh to himself. "Larry, you just don't get it. Next meeting? My boss? We are not company employees. I'm here to show you. Me and you—that's it. We might run into others, but they'll be of our family. It's passed down from generation to generation, as I told you. We do not have meetings or bosses. We are told what to do in our souls, in the fiber of our being, through the smell. Same as a bird is told to fly south. We don't have company parties, no paid vacations, and no get-togethers, unless something big happens where it takes most of us to help clean up. Once, during the Civil War, we all had to band together. Over 51,000 died that day; many hearts at their homes died also. Many could smell death that day, as you can now. But, anyway, we don't have a company. It's more of a calling, and you've been called."

For Larry, that didn't work. He had almost bought into it, but in a flash he had jumped back to wanting no part of it. There must be some way to get out of it. He didn't sign up for this, hadn't filled out anything. So how did he get stuck? He'd lost his life, yet he did not die, nor would he be able to see his son grow up. He was fated to just walk the earth unseen until it was someone's time.

"So, what is in it for me?" he asked, not looking at his father.

Death's time that he could spend with Larry was getting short, but he knew he had to continue to keep his cool. It was not going to get any easier for Larry, especially if he remained obstinate and tried to reject his calling. Maybe he could lighten the air up a bit, but first he had to tell him a thing or two.

"Sad to say, that's what most think these days: what's in it for me? Well, here's one thing: you will get to know the truth about unsolved murders." He chuckled. "You might say, you'll get to see behind the great curtain of Oz. You'll be there. And you'll see who really shot JR."

Larry's puzzled look told Death that he had never seen an episode of *Dallas*, nor did Larry find his attempt at humor funny at all. Larry must have inherited his mother's non-existent sense of humor. They both had been sick the day a sense of humor was handed out.

Before either could say anymore, the screaming sound of screeching tires on the road filled their ears. Both standing outside now, in view of a busy street. They both turned their heads quietly to only see a little girl's body lying lifeless next to what was once a pink bike, but now just a crumpled pile of metal. The pile of metal was wrapped around the front end of a large SUV.

A woman who must have been the girl's mother ran to the small, lifeless body. Larry smelled the scent of death circling the child. The soul was struggling to leave the corpse, but it couldn't break away. It was as if it was waiting for Larry or his dad to touch the body.

Larry rushed over and picked the girl up to help her, and maybe save her. Looking down at the girl he had just picked up, he noticed that it was only her soul he had scooped up in his arms, not her body. He glanced down to see the body still lying on the pavement. The smell was leaving now, as if it too had been released with her soul. The little girl looked at him, eyes wide with shock. "What happened? I was on the ground, like someone pushed me. Who are you?"

Death knew that there was only a short period of time to get the child's soul into the light. He stepped in before Larry could say anything. "I'm a friend, and I'm here to help you see your grandma. I know you have missed her."

"But sir, Nana is in heaven, and I'm not supposed to talk to strangers. I don't know you."

Death had to work fast. This was supposed to be Larry's job, but he'd spent too much time asking questions earlier. He hadn't had time to actually explain how to complete the task. "See that light, child? Look into it, and you will see your Nana, and your friends, and family. Go to them."

The little girl was amazed by the light. She jumped out of Larry's arms and stepped towards it. Before she crossed through the golden doorway, the child turned to look back at the man who had bent down to help her mother with something on the ground. She could hear her mother crying. "My mom says not to leave her," the little girl told Death. "Why is she crying so hard? She only cried this hard when Nana died."

The little girl couldn't see what her mother was hovering over. She didn't realize that it was her own lifeless body. Death knew that he had to get her into the light immediately.

"It's a sad day for your mom. But look in the light. Look at all the people who want to hug you. Go see them. Run to them."

Larry wanted to run to the light too. It seemed so inviting. Again, all he could make out were vague shapes, which looked like arms reaching out. But they weren't reaching out for him.

"Nana," the child cried out, "Nana, granddad, and Uncle Norman!" She ran into the golden glow. As she entered it, she became part of it, and there seemed to be a million arms and hands out, hugging her as she merged with the light, and with them. Then the light slowly faded, like the sun fading behind a cloud. The smell was gone as well, replaced, as with Cindy, by the fragrance of roses, but this time with a touch of candy—better, and happier.

It left Larry with an empty feeling of loss in his heart again. He stood there looking at the fading light, while passers-by gathered around, staring at the body. They didn't see the light or any part of what just happened. They were clueless to it.

Death took Larry by the arm and pulled him off to the side. "The trick is to get them to go into the light quickly, to those who are waiting for them."

Larry nodded. The pain in the mother's eyes was so real, so agonizing. It made him wish he was already a dad, so he could hold his child safely. He wanted to live, to be able to hold his child while it was alive. He wanted to see his child grow, be with him. Yes it would have sad times, but to feel so much love for a child, this he wanted. He whipped his head around and snapped, "I want no part of this. You just took her away from her mother. What kind of a jerk are you? How can you do that?"

Death shook his head. "I'm not a jerk. I'm just doing my job. It was the driver of that SUV who took her life. He didn't see her."

As the EMTs arrived, he led Larry down the sidewalk. "You know, son, all I did was help her pass on, cleaned up the wreckage the driver left behind. But people never see it that way. The way they see us, we're just something to be outdone, beat back; to them it's winning some kind of game to cheat death. The truth is, people kill themselves and others. We don't. We just help them make the jump. Someday, I will reunite the mother and her little girl, but not now. The mother will always be moved to grief when she thinks of her little girl. They are part of each other, and someday they will be one again in the light."

Larry grunted. "Are you trying to talk me into or out of this…job?"

Death looked up at the sky. It was a nice day, with a blue sky full of white small puffy

clouds. Too bad he had to waste it trying to talk
Larry into his calling. He knew Larry must not
be allowed to take Option B or even to learn
about it. "Son, this is not a job you can just quit,
like that, pack it in and walk out of your boring
life. You were born to this, it's your *calling*."

Larry's anger flared up again being told
what to do. He was not going to be coerced into
becoming a killer. "What if I refuse? Will you
go away and never talk to me again? Is that it?
You ran out on us before, my mother and me.
Do it again." He had seen so much today, seen
more than anybody else had ever seen. He just
wanted to go back home to his apartment and
lay next to Pam.

"You aren't allowed to walk away with
all you know now," Death informed him. "I
don't think you fully understand. You really
don't have a choice. You can't go back to what
you had." Both were walking down the street,
but had no destination in mind. Death pulled

313

Larry under the shade of a big oak growing up half into the sidewalk. "Many search their whole life for their 'calling,' only to find out, in the end, that they should have done what they enjoyed and helped other people whenever they could. You are one of the few that really does have a legacy to fulfill. People dream and pray for a purpose in their lives, when all the time they have freedom of choice—what to do and who to love!"

It was Larry's turn to talk now, and he was ready. "What kind of crap is that? Some legacy! Helping people die? Seeing mankind at its worst, killing each other off left and right? Then once they've gone wild and killed one another, we have to help them die—how freaky is that?" He had had enough. It was time to fly. Larry had to get away. He didn't want to hear anything else about his gift, or his legacy, or his calling. He turned and ran, leaving Death under the tree.

He ran off, getting out of sight as soon as he could. He finally reached his home, nearly collapsing as he neared his apartment from shortness of breath. He just wanted to get away from his father. He wanted this crazy day to be over. He wanted to fall asleep and wake up, forgetting about everything he had seen and heard and done. There had to be some way of getting his old life back.

After what seemed like a lifetime of running, Larry finally reached his apartment building. He had never been so glad to see it before. He ran in to see Pam drying her hair after getting out of the shower. He stood in front of her, apologizing for his absence. But she couldn't see him. He waved his arms frantically in front of her face, trying to get her to look at him. Still nothing. He started to reach out to touch her, but pulled back suddenly. He couldn't touch her! If he touched her, she could die. The power of death had not left him. So he stood back, watching and hoping she would suddenly look at him. If she could just see him, he knew things would be all right again. As he stood there staring at her, he heard something behind him. Pam didn't hear it, didn't even raise her head. That can only mean one thing: Death was now in the room, just waiting for a chance to start pressuring him again.

In the other room, Pam's cell phone rang. She went to answer it and disappeared from Larry's view. Now it was only him and his father in the room.

He spoke to his dad without turning around. "This life is not the best it could be, but it's mine. I want to live. I want to be part of it. I want to be a part of Pam's world, of my son's world. I don't want to be a part of your world. I don't have much, but I've worked hard for every bit of it."

He felt a hand on his shoulder as Death came up behind him. He might have died at that moment, but he didn't. Death had touched him, and he was still alive. That only meant one thing: he was Death too. It had already happened to him, without his permission, and there was nothing he could do about it. His eyes filled with tears, it was just so…sad…

"Larry, you really don't belong here anymore. We all want to go back and relive our lives after we've departed. I'm no different. I didn't have a dad either, remember? He showed up one day and told me about all this, the same way I came to you today. It's a lot to take. I would tell you to go to bed and sleep on it. But for you, there is no more sleep. You no longer need it. Or food."

Larry just stood there. He had to find a way out of this mess he was born into. His mind raced as he tried to figure out what to do. He thought of the shaman that Pam had taken him to earlier that week. He shivered as he remembered how the shaman seemed to know who he was even though he never met him before. He only went to see him because he thought he could give him the information that his dad would not tell him. Maybe the shaman could help now. Maybe he would know a way out of this "calling."

Without saying a word, he burst out of the house and took off running down the street. He was running as fast as he could, putting every ounce of his being into it. He was fighting for his life, for his unborn child's right to have a father, and for his wife Pam's right to have a husband. He was running for his life and the life of his family. Many times in his life he was dealt a bad hand of cards, but he knew that the important this was not the cards you're handed, but how you play them. Larry planned on playing this hand out the best he could. He planned on winning. He knew it was hard to beat the house, but sometimes you had to try. And this was one of those times.

Larry ran into the shaman's house as fast as he could, not even stopping to knock. He wondered if the shaman could even see him coming. Maybe he could, who knows, but he had to find out. As he entered the shaman's house, Larry saw him sitting around his fire as if he had never gotten up from Larry's last visit.

The shaman's fire told him a lot of things. He could see things others couldn't see. Some were good, and some were bad. But most of the time he saw good things. He used many different colored items to protect himself from the evil things he sometimes saw. The shaman knew that, if he saw the evil spirits, they could see him as well, so he needed to protect himself at all times. As the shaman stared into the fire, he saw the man that had scared him earlier that week. He saw that the deep part of the woods had found him and he was now one of them; he was now running his way and coming to him.

For a second, he wished he were just a plumber…anything but a shaman with the gift of seeing. He had been born with this gift. He could even remember having it as a child. His gift was better understood by his tribe, but now it seemed that more white people understood and needed his wisdom than his own people…funny how that worked. He was not completely sure, but he believed this young man was named Larry. And Larry was not coming for him, but was coming for help. Just as he thought this, Larry ran into the room, coming to a complete halt with plenty of distance between them, so he would not touch him or any of his sacred objects.

Larry tried to get the words out and catch his breath at the same time. "I'm not here for you. I'm here for me. I need your help."

The shaman did not move or speak, but slowly moved his eyes over him as if to say, "Why me?" Before Larry could answer him, someone else popped in the room. He looked like Larry, except he was an older, more experienced and powerful version. And he hadn't had to run there. He apparently knew of other ways to travel. This other man was clouded by powerful spirits. The terrified shaman decided that it was time to kick up the prayers, so he threw some special colored dust into the fire. The flames turned blue, and both men moved backed away from the shaman.

"I desperately need your help," Larry started. He quickly told the shaman that the man standing next to him was his father. He recounted the whole story of his day, while the shaman sat and stared into the fire, occasionally tossing different items in, making the color of the fire change periodically. He wasn't even sure if the shaman was really listening to him, but it felt good to share his traumatic experiences with someone. And to someone who could actually see and hear him.

Larry waited for what felt like an eternity for the shaman to respond to his story. Death was standing next to him, with his head hanging down silently. Finally, the shaman tossed something into the fire, and a green flash arose amongst a trail of smoke. He turned to Larry. "You can get out of it. You have not truly become it yet, but the cost is high. The pain is even more."

Larry looked over at his father, searching for his reaction. His father's head was still hanging low, purposefully staring at the ground to avoid eye contact with his son. But he eventually nodded slowly, which told Larry that there was an alternative. The shaman was correct. His father knew it would be very painful, so much so he found it unbearable to tell Larry; he was just hoping all he had to do was go along and agree with the shaman's advice. He didn't want to be to the one to tell Larry about it, or worse, to actually see his son go through with it.

Larry had been raised to understand the true meaning of freedom; however a person decided to react to a situation or statement, whether with their words or their actions. This was a reflection of a person's true freedom. Larry knew he had to get the shaman and his father to tell him what he had to do, so he could use his freedom of choice to decide the best course of action for him. Larry was at the point of begging. "What is it? Shouldn't I be allowed to weigh the cost myself? Shouldn't I get to make my own judgment? What pain? Do I get eaten by some beast and ride around in their stomach until I change my mind? Turn to salt? What?"

The shaman points to Larry's father. "It's his job to tell you. I cannot. Please leave now and don't come back. Come back only when it's my time to go. You give an old man a scare each time you show up. I think you are here for me."

Larry knew he had overstayed his welcome with the shaman. It was time to go. He also knew that the only option he had was to talk to his father, Death himself. As he retreated from the shaman's house, his father softly grabbed his arm and led him out. He wanted to tell him that they needed to go out for some fresh air to break the tension. He wanted to seem nonchalant. But he knew his son would not fall for that again. He would have to break the news to him once they were outside. He wanted to be away from others when he delivered the news he so desperately did not want to tell his son.

Chapter Fourteen
Rules of the Universe

Larry and his dad found a bench to sit on next to the shaman's house. It was only a short walk away, but it seemed like years to Larry. The anticipation was killing him. He was finally going to find a loophole and get himself out of this mess.

Larry's father began to speak. "Larry, first of all, by saying no to something, you say yes to something else. So, no matter what action you take, you'll never get to know your son and you can't go back to your wife. But that is just a small part of it. I was hoping to get to know you as I got to know my father, but that will be my loss. If I tell you what you have to do, your life on earth would be a personal hell. Are you sure you really want to know? I really think you should trust me on this one, because you don't."

But Larry had to know. He had to judge for himself. "I have to know, no matter what it is. If I choose not to do it, I can someday tell my son when it's his turn to join why I made that decision. Dad, has anybody ever decided not to do it?"

Larry's dad knew he had to list the disclaimers first while he still had Larry's full and undistracted attention. "It's different for everyone. All I can say is, no one has made it through your ordeal, but they have made it through their ordeal. I'll tell you, if you really want to know." He now felt like he was dragging it out, but he had to get this point across before it was too late. "Larry, I am kind of enjoying just talking to you, but I will not enjoy telling you what I have to say. Well, that's part of it. I can't really tell you exactly what you will have to go through because, for each person, it's different. You will even have to experience a different hell than I do."

Larry nodded as if he wasn't confused.

"First of all, you will live seven years of personal hell. Every month, something new will infect you. The only thing that is consistent is that people will dislike you. In fact, they won't even care enough to hate you. No one will talk to you or speak to you, but they will yell at you. On sight, they won't want anything to do with you. No matter how nice or pleasant a person is, when they see you, they'll do anything to get you out of their life."

Upon hearing this, Larry's face aged about fifteen years. The news was almost too much to comprehend. "Seven years?" was all he could ask.

Death took advantage of Larry's speechlessness to fill in more details before all the questions began again. "For seven years, you will not hold down a job. You will be kicked out of homeless shelters. You will be covered in boils. You no longer enjoy the taste of food; it will taste and smell like vomit. A wide range of things will happen to you. And just when you think you have figured it all out and seen it all, something new will set in."

Larry's dad wasn't sure that his son comprehended the gravity of what he was trying to express. He knew he couldn't use words to express how painful life would be if Larry chose to avoid his calling. He could see it in Larry's eyes—he was only hearing the part about getting out of it; he was not really understanding or weighing the cost. Larry reminded him of himself those many years ago. When you're part of the human race, you tend to focus on the immediate advantages. You can't see far enough into the future to realize the costs that come along with it. Get it now, pay later, and with any luck the later would go away. And he knew that this was what Larry was thinking. He wasn't concerned with his future or the price he had to pay.

Larry looked at his father. "And if I go along with this plan, I would be free from the calling?"

Larry's dad did not know how to tell him. He did not know how to explain or make Larry understand that his life would never be the same. He didn't know how to explain how once his choice was made, he could never go back. Most people have this false feeling that each day is the same. They go on with their lives, doing the same thing every day until something major happens. When someone dies or when they lose their job, then they have to admit that each day is different—each day is new and will not be the same as before. For Larry, this was that day. He had to admit sooner or later that nothing would ever be the same again after this point.

But the worst part was that Death hadn't yet told Larry about the worst part, about what happened at the end of the seven years.

Larry did not say anything or ask more questions. In fact, he didn't want to know any more. He waited for his dad to talk. If he wanted to share more, then he could, but for now he would just be still and not ask any more questions. Once he looked at his dad, he could see that he was going to tell him more.

When Death didn't continue, Larry considered what he had said. Okay, seven years of hell. But then it's over, right? In the eighth year, he could make friends again. He could find a job. He could return to Pam and get to know their son. Wouldn't seven years of torture be worth that?

Larry started to smile. Maybe it wouldn't be as bad as he thought.

But no sooner had that thought crossed his mind, than his dad resumed. "Larry, you don't understand. There is one final thing you need to know. You have the bloodline…you can't have kids."

"But I have a son, or I will. So, I don't need anymore."

"Again, you don't understand. You can't have kids. You have one last chance to change your mind, or your son will be taken."

Before he could finish Larry jumped in. "What the hell are you saying?"

Larry's dad didn't have to answer, but he did. "I think you understand what I'm saying. You just don't want to hear it. And before you ask, no, you can't get out of this part. I know you just want an easy out. You have two paths to take, and you have twelve hours to make up your mind."

No, Larry thought to himself. *There has to be another way.* Maybe he could refuse to choose.

But his father anticipated this. "Remember, one of the great lies humans tell themselves is 'I did not pick this, or it was not my choice.' But sometimes we make a choice by not doing anything at all. Therefore, if you choose not to do anything, you pick to be tested for seven years. There is no turning back."

But Death could see that Larry still wasn't accepting the gravity of the situation. He knew his son would choose the path of least resistance; he would simply give up. He had to try one final time. He had to make him see things clearly before it was too late. He needed to tell him every last detail.

"Larry before make your decision, you need to know something else. If you decide to follow your calling, you must complete the required tasks. You can't shirk your duties. It's not a job; it's a calling. No weekends off. No going home to the family at night. You live in the shadows of humans' sights, just out of view until the last day of their lives. You need to get over yourself."

But Larry's mind only could come up with, "How do I know you're telling the truth?"

Death was getting irritated. "You don't. Go ahead and try refusing to work and see how long you can last. I'm tired of trying to help you. I've told you what's good for you based on thousands of years of experience. But I can see you don't believe me. From what you've seen, how can you not believe I'm telling you the truth?"

Larry had given up trying to talk to his dad. His mind was made up, and he was done with it. He decided he would just wait and see what happened to him.

He had learned to wait things out in grade school. All his teachers had said, "If you can't listen here, it will only get harder in high school." But once he got to high school, he only found out that things were actually easier—he could pick his classes, choose his teachers, skip school. But the high school teachers only repeated what his other teachers had said: "college is really hard, so you better listen and pay attention." But, once again, college proved even easier than high school. Somehow he felt the situation with his father was the same way. Well, it wasn't going to work on him today.

Larry's dad sensed Larry pulling away. He had one last chance to stress the significance of his choice before he lost him completely. "Remember, you have twelve hours before it starts. Oh, and one more thing. Good luck son. Just so you know, everyone tries to cheat death. You're no different. In the end, it always goes the same way."

Larry shrugged. He was playing the role of the obstinate child. "What's so wrong with Hell anyways?"

Death could see that Larry was just toying with him. However, he was his son. He decided to humor him. "From what I see, it's a place to pay for your debts. If, during your life, you hurt or wronged someone, you get to feel their pain in Hell. You don't have any power over it. You just have to live with it."

"Okay, so what's Heaven like then?"

Death sighed. As the questions continued, he decided provided answers. At the very least, it was a chance to build up trust between the two of them. And he would definitely need that bond later. Sooner or later, Larry would need his dad. "Heaven is where you feel the love and care you gave during your lifetime. To feel loved as you loved." That was the best way he could explain it, the best he understood it from looking though the doorway. But he knew it was like seeing an entire ocean through a keyhole.

Larry decided he had had enough. "This is crap. I'm going home. I'm done with you. Go back home. I was happy without you. I didn't know any better, and want it that way again." Before his dad could say anything, Larry popped off the bench and walked away, leaving his dad behind. He glanced back, but only to give a look of disbelief before he started his walk home. *What crap*, he thought. It was time to get out of here and call it a day. He would simply go back home to Pam, have something to eat, watch some mindless TV, and go to bed. That was the only real solution to the day's craziness.

Larry's dad remained on the bench and watched his son walk away. As Larry walked under some of the overhanging streetlights, they dimmed and went out. He noticed that Larry was too busy in his own world to see this.

Larry was musing to himself. Funny how earlier that day he didn't even know who his father was. Now he knew it all. He knew why his father had left. He knew why he felt different from others. He should be happy. But it was a lot of information to process in a day, and Larry just wanted his old life back.

But Larry didn't understand that he could not have his old life back because it was forever changed. Yes, he would get used to it, but not over it. In a way, it was like the death of someone in your own life—your mother or a friend. You only get used to it; you never lose the pain, or really get over it. You just got accustomed to it over time.

Death knew that it was time to let Larry go. He had a lot to think about. The gravity of everything was sure to sink in soon. Apparently, Larry needed to see what happens when he doesn't play along with the powers that be, the rules of the universe. Everybody does what he or she has to get over something like this, even if it was just blocking it out.

Chapter Fifteen
First Step

Larry took a nice and slow walk home because he wanted to make sure his dad did not follow him. He also just wanted to clear his head and have some time to think it all over. As he walked into his apartment building, he glanced up to see that there was a cop at the top of the stairs standing just outside his neighbor's apartment. With all that went on that day, he still could not believe he had forgotten about her. The cop must be here because they found her body. Now Larry was walking in, and the cop was going to want to talk to him. Most likely, he would think he had something to do with it. Larry thought about ducking out, but it was too late; the cop had already seen him and made eye contact with him. Regardless, the cop would not believe what Larry had been through that day. Suddenly Larry thought about being in her apartment earlier that day when she had passed on and wondered if he had touched anything. He hoped not. He thought about his fingerprints scattered around her apartment. *Oh, crap*!

As Larry got closer to the cop, it seemed he was just doing another routine death report on the old lady. When he spotted Larry walking, you could see that he was not at all surprised to see him. The cop wondered what Larry's excuse would be this time. The cop imagined Larry saying, "Mister, I didn't kill them. I just always seem to be there." He also wondered where the weird key chain with the stone was. He knew Larry always had it on him. The cop was determined to get answers to all his questions this time.

"So what the hell are you doing here?" the cop asked.

Larry had to stay and talk now, but he was determined to keep it short. "I live next door. I was just coming home from a walk."

The cop did not believe him. "Let me guess…you had nothing to do with this and you just happen to live next door."

Larry thought about it. He *did* have something to do with her death, but how do you tell a cop you're Death, and that you only took her life so she could pass on. Larry imagined himself with the cop on his back and his face planted into the carpet floor if he voiced that thought out loud. There was a part of Larry that wished the cop could just lock him up for a long, long time and toss the key away.

The cop was very good at his job and could often "feel" when a person was lying. He knew something was up; he could tell that Larry was not sharing everything. As a cop, he had that feeling many times before, but this time it was over the top. Larry was just flat out lying to him. He was not going to give up easily. "Let's see here…what you are saying is that you just happen to be someplace when someone passes on, and now you live next door to it?"

Larry kept walking to his apartment like nothing was wrong. "Yeah, nothing weird about that."

The cop wanted to take him in, but, once again, he knew he had nothing. He knew, if he could just get some time alone with Larry and bring him in for questioning, he would be able to get to the bottom of it. The room was still and eerily quiet until the cop's radio spoke out. It was his wife. She worked at the station; she liked the fact that she could keep a close eye on him. The radio blared out, "The parents of the child who died in the hit and run today are here at the station and ready to talk to you. Can you come to the station?"

The cop grabbed Larry as he passed by, scaring Larry, which was what he wanted to do. He pushed Larry up to the wall before leaning in and telling him, "I'll be back to talk to you. You live here, right?" He nodded towards Larry's front door.

Larry moved his head as if to say yes.

"I'll be back then. Don't go anyplace or do anything, and I stress the anything part. I'm not going to get called on another death am I?"

Larry shook his head. The cop released his hold on him and walked towards the exit. *Will this day never end?*

As Larry picked himself up and walked to his front door, he realized he had totally forgotten about the little girl who died in the car crash earlier that day. It was sad that something so tragic had slipped his mind so easily. So many things like that had happened that day. Larry just wanted it to end. Some days, the end comes oh so soon. But today, the end couldn't come soon enough.

Larry walked into his apartment and practically fell into the first thing he saw: a chair by the door. It was a nice, well-used chair, big and soft, and it was doing exactly what it was made for, supporting all of his weight because it was too much for him to carry now. He thought about all the things that had happened to him that day and quickly deduced it was all a bunch of crap. He couldn't believe that anything his father said would ever come to pass...his father was just trying to scare him into believing it. He sat in the chair and fell to sleep. He did not dream because he was too tried. He just slept hard that night, which seemed like forever.

The next morning Larry was still sleeping in the chair when Pam walked out of the bedroom. She was surprised to see Larry asleep in the chair. It was unlike him to sleep anywhere besides their bed, except, of course, when she forced him to sleep on the couch.

Yesterday seemed like such a long day, so she had slept in too, and it was late in the morning. It was time to get Larry up, so she walked over and kissed him on the head; this usually woke him up fast. He was always ready for more skin to skin time. As usual, her kiss worked like a charm, and Larry's eyes popped right open. Larry looked down at his watch and noticed that he had been asleep for some time…a long time in fact. It was just two minutes shy from when he had arrived home twelve hours ago, the time that all hell was supposed to break loose.

He thought about all those people who predicted national disasters or the end of the world. Everyone would sit and watch their clocks, but, eventually, nothing would happen. He believed this would be one of those times. He was determined he wouldn't see anything. Besides, Pam had just kissed him, and he was hoping it would lead to better things.

Pam decided it was time to cool Larry down. "I have to pee for two now, me and the baby have to go."

When she came back from the bathroom she asked, "Larry, where did you go last night? I couldn't find you. Cindy from next door, she, she..." Pam quickly leaned into Larry and gave him a hug as she told him their next door neighbor had died yesterday. "I thought something happened to you. We are going to have a family now. You just can't run off. Don't scare me like that again. Stay here; I'll be right back, I want to get a drink of water."

After Pam left the room, Larry's alarm went off on his watch. He didn't even remember setting it. The alarm was set to the exact time Larry was supposed to make a decision about his future—to become Death or be plagued for the rest of his life. He paused, waiting for something to happen. He felt no different, no pain. Just as he thought—nothing. All was good. *What a crack pot that man was. I bet he wasn't even my dad*, Larry thought. *Well let's just enjoy the day, and many more to come.*

Pam walked back into the room with a bright smile on her face. This was it, Larry thought, he had won. Pam had gotten a glass of ice water before returning to talk with Larry. As she moved closer to Larry, he could see a wave of pain, or disgust, as if she just bit into a worm while eating an apple. She looked up at Larry. Her face grew really sour. The glass slipped out of her hand and shattered on the floor. This was so unlike her, to make a mess like this. Larry just sat in the chair, seeing her sour face turn to anger now. Her eyes became completely black, as if something evil had entered into them. They were the same color as the darkest part of stone in his key ring. It was like the soul of the stone had entered her, and it was now looking at him with its cold eyes and heart. He had spent hours looking at the stone, somehow thinking it was almost alive, and now he understood that it was.

Pam was not sure what came over her, but Larry was really upsetting her. Not the fake kind of upset that she pulled on him many of times before, but this was for real. She was not sure why, but she was enraged. Then a thought popped in her mind: *what a jerk for skipping out last night*. She was going to lay it on him, "Larry, Why did you skip out last night? I can't believe I married you! Your lazy ass never wants to get a real job so we can have a real life, a real house, a real family...not this freaky life. Why can't you be normal?"

Larry had never seen his wife so upset. Sometimes she pretended she was upset, and he played along, but this time it was for real. He needed to cool her down. "Pam you're upset. Think about the baby and what it can do to the unborn child."

Larry thought the baby thing up on the fly, and it seemed to work for a second, until she stepped one step closer to him. Then the stone cold eyes glared at him, with even more hate than before. She was yelling, but Larry had never heard his wife use that particular tone before. She sounded nothing like herself. He could tell she was very, very upset. "You are such a jerk! I am sick of you! You need to get the hell out of here! I don't want the baby to know anything about you. Get out, you freak!"

Larry's first thought was to leave the apartment and give her some time to cool down, but that didn't make any sense either since that's why she was upset with him in the first place. He felt trapped and didn't know what to do. Then he thought about what his father had told him last night. Once twelve hours had passed, people would hate him. *OH NO*, Larry thought, *it was really happening*.

The closer Pam got to him, the more she seemed to hate him. He knew that it was the same color of the stone, but was the stone somehow controlling her? He stepped away from Pam to see if she would cool down some. "Pam, you're just upset again. It always goes away. I'll take a walk around the block and let you cool down a little. It's okay." He hoped that would help, and, as he stepped away a little more, Pam did seem a little calmer. She then stepped in to give Larry a hug, and her eyes went dark again.

"I told you to get out of here! Now… and don't come back!"

Larry decided to leave. He needed some time and space to decide his next move. And it wasn't hard to figure out that nothing good was going to come from him staying at his apartment. He started heading for the door, but then he got a severe cramp. He dropped to the floor. His insides felt like they were turning inside out, and the pain was unbearable. What was worse was the thought that everything his Dad had told him the night before seemed to be coming true. It was going to be a long seven years.

"Pam, I'm in pain. My stomach hurts." Larry felt like he wanted to just stick something in his side like a garden hose, to siphon all the water or air out and relieve the pressure. She stepped closer to him. But instead of helping him, she started pushing his body closer to the door with her foot, kicking him, getting him to move. Then she yelled, "It's called bloating and cramps you idiot. Women have it every month during their period... live with it and GET OUT! I just want you out of my sight!"

When Larry got closer to the front door, she ran to the door and opened it. She just wanted him out and gone from her life. He might be the father of her child, but she could find a good dad for the baby. This way, she and the baby would not have to put up with him and his weird crap anymore.

As Larry crawled out of the apartment door, Pam stopped kicking and pushing with her feet. She paused for a moment and looked at Larry laying on the floor in agony. Larry looked back at her, waiting and hoping to see some trace of love that he knew his wife had for him. And for a split second he saw the Pam he knew; he saw love in her eyes. But just as quickly, her eyes were once again filled with anger, and she slammed the door leaving Larry alone on the ground outside of the apartment.

Larry slowly stood up and walked outside. He was still in pain, but it had either slowed or he was getting accustomed to it. He wasn't sure where to go. His mind turned to the shaman. Maybe he could help. Maybe he had something that could fix the situation. He decided he had better hurry to find out before he was hit with something else.

Larry couldn't believe what was happening. If it hadn't been for the pain, he wouldn't believe it. Pam was prone to bad moods, and pregnancy was known to do crazy things to women's bodies. Maybe this was all just a big coincidence. Maybe it didn't have anything to do with his father.

Larry walked around the corner of the building and came across a pair of young boys, kicking a soccer ball back and forth. They were smiling and laughing. But as Larry moved closer to them, their faces changed. They glared angrily at Larry. They left the ball in the middle of the sidewalk and looked around. They spotted some stones and a stick laying next to them. At the same time, they started picking up the rocks and hurled them at Larry.

As Larry ducked to avoid the onslaught, he realized that this was not a coincidence. Something strange was happening. The boys were overcome with hate for Larry. "Get out of here, you weird man," they shouted at him. "Mom, a weird man is bugging us."

At that, a woman appeared in the doorway of the building they were in front of. Larry recognized her. He passed her on his way to work every day. Sometimes, they would chat about the weather or a television program from the night before. She saw the boys throwing rocks at Larry and started to instruct the boys to stop. But then she made eye contact with Larry. Her eyes glazed over as Pam's had. He had never felt so much anger, at one person before. She had forgotten about telling the boys to stop. If anything, she wanted to tell them that they needed to throw more items at him. She grabbed a shovel lying in the flowerbed next to her and flung it at Larry's head. "Get out of here, you freak! Police! Police!"

Larry turned and ran the other way. He knew it was time to get out of there. He was sure that the same old cop was going to show up sometime soon. He was already suspicious of Larry. If he showed up while the kids and their mom were screaming at him, he would jump to all sorts of conclusions.

As if the world was conspiring against him, Larry rounded the corner and ran straight into the very police officer he was working so hard to avoid. Larry tumbled to the ground and a barrage of stones came flying after him. The officer was shocked, to say the least. He turned his attention to the boys and their mother. *What in the hell?*

Larry scampered to his feet and took off in a sprint down the road. The cop decided he should pursue him—he had to have done something to warrant getting pelted with rocks.

Larry was racing down the street. The cop was close at his heels. And the boys and their mother were going along for the ride, continuing to shout obscenities and throw whatever they could find. Larry was easily pulling away from the cop until his side started hurting again. *Seriously?* thought Larry. He ducked into an alley and hid behind a garbage can. Thankfully, the cop didn't see him and passed him by. Larry remained hidden for some time. His side was killing him, and he was out of breath. After what seemed like an eternity,

Larry crawled out from his hiding place. He looked around to make sure everyone was gone. The coast was clear.

Larry clutched his sides as he made his way down the street. It felt as if his insides were on fire. Maybe he should try to make it to the hospital. The head nurse was one of Pam's close friends. She had always been nice to Larry, despite his eccentricities. In fact, if he hadn't already been married to Pam, he might have asked her out. She had the special gift of making everyone around her feel good. Except Pam, of course, who called her "Mother Teresa" behind her back and taunted her for her selflessness.

Larry stumbled along his way to the hospital. He clutched his side as he walked through the front door. He thought that something might pop out of his side at any moment. The nurse was busy waiting on someone else, so Larry took his place in line. She was being especially pleasant to the man in front of him. The man was complaining about something trivial, but the nurse was patiently coaxing him. He left contentedly.

When it was Larry's turn, the nurse looked up with a smile. But the sunshine in her eyes quickly turned to stone when she saw Larry. He decided to push on, though. It was her job to help people, after all. Even if she didn't like them. "I need some pain killers," Larry whined. "About seven years of them. Please help me." With that, he fell to the floor.

"Larry, get out of here," the nurse spat at him. "The hospital is for real people who need real help, not druggies like you."

All Larry was able to choke out was "but I need a doctor."

"Not any more. Get out of here, or I'll call the police. You can get your drugs some other place."

Softly, Larry whined, "Please help me."

From behind him, Larry heard a noise. It sounded like someone was moving in a leather seat. It sounded like a rather large someone based on the sounds of the chair. Larry turned to see a very large man coming his way, with a look intent on murder in his eyes. In fact, Larry noticed for the first time that there was an entire waiting room full of people whose eyes were intensely focused on him. The large man was moving towards Larry. Still crouching on the ground, Larry tried to give his best "puppy dog" look, hoping that it might deter the man from killing him.

The man leaned over Larry, fists clenched. His voice was gruff and full of hate. "Get out of here… now… as she said."

Without thinking, Larry spoke back. "But I just want help," he timidly cried. Immediately, Larry wished he could take it back, but it was too late. Larry could see from the man's face that he was a man of few words.

357

Larry was going to be the outlet for his anger today. The man grabbed Larry by the back of his shirt, as if he was a little kitten one-tenth the size of his counterpart. With his other hand, he opened the hospital door, and tossed Larry to the street like a rag doll. Larry heard cheering from the inside of the hospital, as everyone applauded the man's actions.

It was crystal clear that his father had been right. There was no way Larry could deny that now. He slowly stood up, still clutching his side, and made his way down the street, carefully avoiding close contact with anyone nearby. He had one last hope—the shaman. It was a long shot, but Larry had to take the chance. If nothing else, maybe the shaman would feed him to his fire and put him out of his misery.

The intense pain made Larry realize that, up to this point, he had never really been sick. He had a new understanding of what some people went through on a daily basis. It's easy to be in a good mood when you feel good, but, when your body hurts, you have to work a lot harder. Everything becomes a struggle, even simple tasks like standing. Larry was seeing things from a new perspective. He thought about his own problems. Sure, he had been ostracized as a child. Sure, his dad hadn't been around. Sure, he was teased mercilessly. But none of those things could hold a candle to how he was feeling now. He was sorry he had wasted so much of his life feeling sorry for himself.

He was deep in thought and failed to notice someone coming towards him out of the corner of his eye. He had let his guard down. Maybe he could move somewhere with less people. North Dakota? Canada? Antarctica?

With that thought, the person next to him touched him on the shoulder. Larry cringed, waiting for the pain. Everyone was looking for an opportunity to hurt him. Larry closed his eyes, but no pain came. He tentatively peered at the figure. Then he heard his dad's voice: "you okay, son?"

Larry opened his eyes and looked at his father. He was confused. "I can see you, and it hasn't been seven years yet. What's going on?"

Larry was relieved that the pain left him as soon as he saw his father. His father was grateful too, since no father wants to see his son in pain. "I had a break," Death informed him. "I thought I'd come and check up on you. Only you can see me. How are you feeling?"

Larry slowly nodded his head to signal that he was all right.

"Some people live with that hurt or pain every day. Some even have double the pain. You have about another second before the next one hits you. Remember, no one will help you, son. So just stay as far away from others as you can."

Larry didn't say anything. It was just good to hear a voice that wasn't pissed at him and see someone who wasn't trying to hurt him. He decided that he would stand there and enjoy the pleasant change. Before he met someone else who would haze him. Or before one of his pains took over again.

Finally he asked, "seven years?" He started to rub his eyes. "My eyes are getting kind of blurry. It feels like there's some sort of film over them. I can almost see you, but not clearly. And there's a weird pressure behind them." As Larry was speaking, the pressure behind his eyes began to spread to the rest of his head. It was a cross between a steady pounding and a blinding stab.

"It's a migraine," his father informed him. "Your mother used to get them. It causes paralysis and weakness on one side of the body, mimicking a stroke. In a little while, you're going to feel drained of energy and may experience sensitivity to light and sound. But there's worse to come. So save your energy for the really bad spells. I have to go now."

Larry couldn't see his dad leave, but he could sense that he was gone. *Really bad spells*? Larry wanted to cry. He had to get to the shaman's house, and quickly.

Though his eyes were blurry, he could make out the figure of a woman working in the garden in the backyard of a house. Larry tried to move out of the woman's line of sight, but bumped into something. It was the remains of a very old car. He sprawled out onto the hood, and the noise caught the woman's attention. He tried to disengage himself from the car, but got tangled in something on the ground. He could see the woman making her way towards him. This wasn't going to be good.

The woman saw Larry tangled in a garden hose, leaning against the car. She immediately thought that he was trying to break into it. There weren't many homeless people in town, but she was sure that's what Larry was by his appearance. And, indeed, he was extremely disheveled from the day's events and moving awkwardly from his impaired vision. The woman grabbed a garden hoe and stomped towards Larry.

"Get out of here, you drunk!" she shouted, as she shook the hoe at him. She might have been old, but she could still give him a good cut with it if she had to. She was sure he was some miscreant come to steal her property, or worse. Well, she would show him that even an old lady could protect what was hers.

"I'm not drunk," Larry mumbled. "I just don't feel good." He worked furiously to disengage himself, but every movement seemed to trap him even tighter to the spot.

The woman wasn't buying it. "Yeah, right. Next you'll say you need money for your medicine. But I know what your medicine it—

the Devil's booze! You won't find any of that devil's spirit around here, you drunk. So, be gone with you!" She was happy to know her son never drank in college. He would come home late, sure, but the next morning he was always very thirsty, so he could not have drank the night before. No one would drink that much water the next day if he had had anything to drink the night before.

Larry had learned his lesson from the man at the hospital: he needed to move. People were really trying to hurt him. Luckily, his eyes started to clear enough that he was able to unwrap the hose from his legs. Two seconds before the old woman swung the hoe at his back, he had gotten free and was running down the street. The hoe whacked the hood of the car, leaving a massive dent. She sure was strong for her age!

Larry made it two blocks before he had to stumble into an alley to vomit. He wasn't sure whether it was the adrenaline, or the stress, or the headache, or just another plague. But he stood heaving into a corner for nearly five minutes. When the wave of nausea passed, Larry looked around. He noticed an old shed at the end of the alley. It hadn't been painted in years. The roof was caving in and the exterior was rusting. Larry wasn't sure whether it was abandoned or just in disrepair. He figured he would check it out. Anyplace to hide him from passersby with stones, and hoes, and those eerie black eyes.

He walked inside. Aside from a broken-down lawnmower, the shed was empty. He grabbed the tarp off the machine and laid it on the floor. Not the most comfortable situation, but it was like Heaven after every place else he visited that day. He plopped down on the tarp and attempted to sleep. Maybe his migraine would go away if he could catch a few hours of rest.

Larry slept soundly, as if he was dead to the world. When he finally woke, he wasn't sure what time it was or how long he had been asleep. But then again, he also didn't have time to care. Larry had been woken up by the sound of someone trying to open the front door of the shed.

The shed's windows were covered in grime, but Larry could just make out the figure of a man fiddling with the door. Larry looked around for a place to hide. Unfortunately, there was nothing around, and there was only one door. To make things worse, Larry heard a bark. A dog? Really?

The man finally got the door open. Sure enough, he had a large black lab on a leash with him. Its fur was standing up, and it was barking harshly at Larry, who was still half asleep on the tarp. The dog was pulling at the leash, lunging towards Larry. Apparently dogs hated the sight of him as well.

Larry rose to his feet, trying to determine whether or not he could dart past the pair and make a break for the door. The man seemed to sense his thoughts. "Get the hell out of here. Sleep it off someplace else! Get out now, or I'll let her loose on you!"

Larry started to tell the man he was sorry, but he knew it wouldn't do any good. Anything he might say would only infuriate the man further. Larry took a big step towards the door, trying to avoid the angry canine.

But as Larry took his first step, his leg gave out under his weight. A strange snapping sound accompanied his fall. The dog was pulling at the leash, inching closer by the second. Larry knew he had to get up and go, but the pain was excruciating. He wondered whether he should just stay down and let the dog take care of him. The old man didn't seem to care that Larry was unable to walk. He likely thought it was just the aftereffects of a bottle of booze. "That's your bones falling apart, from drinking so damn much! Stop drinking, you jerk!"

Larry wished it was that easy. He looked at the man pleadingly, but to no avail. His eyes had turned to stone black. No remorse.

Larry leveraged himself on to the lawnmower and pulled upright. He limped slowly towards the door, the dog barking the whole time. The man stood aside, letting him pass by.

Once again, Larry's thoughts turned to the shaman. All of his previous plans had backfired on him. He hoped that the shaman wouldn't freak out and toss him in the fire. But he didn't have another choice at this point.

Chapter Sixteen
Behind the Veil of the Great Oz

Larry took as many back alleys as he could find, attempting to keep away from people as much as he could. At one point, he heard the cop talking to someone in the street. He immediately recognized the officer's voice—he had grown to know that voice too well. And he was definitely the last person Larry wanted to run into at the moment.

He finally arrived at the shaman's house. He peered around—no one seemed to be nearby. He listened at the front door. When he didn't hear anything, he slowly opened the door and crept inside. A few individuals were seating in the front room, which had been turned into a waiting room. *Crap*! He had to make it past them before their eyes shifted and they tried to kill him. He bolted for the back room with all the speed his gimpy leg could provide.

Fortunately, the shaman was alone in the back. Just as he began to speak, a sharp pain struck Larry's lower back. He locked up immediately and fell to the floor once again. He was writhing in pain at the shaman's feet. Sweat covered his face, and his body contorted into shapes Larry hadn't even dreamed of being in before. Tears streamed from his eyes. He didn't know if he would be able to get out the words to ask for help.

However, the shaman recognized what was going on. "Somehow I knew you'd be back," he sighed. "It looks like a disc has gone out in your lower back. Pretty painful, huh?" He nonchalantly turned from Larry and rummaged around a shelf. He chose a vial that was full of a viscous yellow concoction. He tossed it to Larry. "Most of the time, this would do the trick. But, in your case, I'm not sure…"

Larry was thankful for even the least attempt at aid. He fumbled with the lid and poured the liquid down his back. For a moment, the pain was gone. But then it came back with redoubled intensity. Larry screamed.

"Just as I thought," replied the shaman.

"What's happening to me?" Larry managed to eke out. "First my head, then my eyes, then my legs, and now my back…"

The shaman nodded. "Your body is dying."

Larry was confused, to say the least. His father had told him that he would never die, but the shaman seemed to be pretty sure that he was.

The old man sensed his confusion. "Your body is dying, Larry. But not you. It's part of the price you paid. You are feeling all the pains that people deal with day to day. Diseases are free to attack you at will. Soon the pains of death will also start. You will feel what it's like to die of bone cancer, but not die. What's it like to die of sickle cell anemia, heart attack, emphysema, pneumonia, be burned to death. All of this you will suffer, but you will never die. But the pains will continue. Some days you'll be lucky and only have bad acid reflux. Others, not so lucky. The one consolation is that you will experience the symptoms one at a time, so no two things will occur simultaneously."

Larry didn't think that was a very good loophole.

"I cannot help you," the shaman continued, "or I, too, will feel the same pain as you. All I can do is give you this key. It opens the door to an apartment below this house. You can use the apartment, as long as you stay away from me and my guests."

The shaman could see the pain in Larry's eyes, and he really did want to help. But he also needed to think of his own safety. And his safety—indeed his life—depended on getting Larry away from him. He knew there would be a price to pay for harboring the Death's son, but it was in his nature to help others. Just as Larry's calling was sensing death, his calling was healing others. "You can get to the apartment by the back door. But go, now, before the others see you. I don't want a riot in the middle of my shop."

Larry dutifully picked up the key and followed the shaman towards the back door. His lower back was still pulsating, but he could walk steadily as long as he hunched over. The shaman peered out into the back yard and waved at Larry, signaling that the coast was clear. Larry stealthily wound around the house to the basement door. The pain in his back was beginning to subside. He almost cried tears of joy when he opened the old door.

Inside was a small, musty apartment. The shaman must have been using it for storage, but it seemed like a palace to Larry at the moment. He lowered himself into an ancient faded recliner that reeked of mothballs and wriggled around until he found a position that didn't put too much pressure on his lower back. The darkness of the room encompassed him, and Larry quickly fell to sleep.

When he woke up the next morning, Larry wasn't sure what time it was. Then again, did time really matter with seven years of pain? His back seemed to be better, but he was bitterly cold. He wondered whether this was another plague, or if the basement wasn't insulated.

He wasn't sure why the shaman had let him stay. He was fairly sure, though, that the shaman could get into trouble for doing so. Larry tried not to think about that.

"So, what's on the menu for today?" Larry asked himself. "Malaria, typhoid, or encephalitis?"

He glanced around the room. Boxes of garage-sale items filled most of the floor space, a pile of rolled up scrolls and old newspapers spilled out from the corner, and several wall hangings leaned against the walls. Next to the recliner, there was a small end table covered in an inch of dust and a pile of books. Larry flipped through the stack, trying to find something to occupy his time until the next wave of disease hit.

He chuckled to himself at the irony when he found a book titled, *Diseases Known to Mankind*. Had this been a gift from the shaman? Or just another strange coincidence? Either way, it was definitely going to come in handy over the next seven years. He flipped the book open. Unfortunately, the subtitled was "12,420 Disease Categories in ICD-10."

Perfect. Larry did some quick math in his head. He figured that, if he was to experience every single disease in the book, he would be blighted with at least four different maladies every single day over the next seven years.

Larry let the book fall from his hand and put his weight back into the recliner. He was beginning to get dizzy and starting to shake. He rummaged through one of the nearby boxes and found a fraying afghan. He shook a cobweb off of it and then covered his head, even though he knew it likely wouldn't stave off the chill. He wondered what disease he was starting now, but wasn't sure if he wanted to know.

As his eyes glazed over, a shape appeared in front of Larry. It was out of focus, but started to become clearer. It was his father. Larry made a mental note to keep his father's otherworldly mode of transportation in mind so he didn't have a heart attack every time he popped in.

Larry's dad was happy to see him. He was hoping that Larry had experienced enough over the last day to change his mind. He knew that Larry wouldn't be able to take much more. "Son," he said gently, "with a touch of my hand, this can all go away. All the pain will be over. All the suffering. All the fear. Just touch my hand, and you can take your rightful place beside me. You can do what you're fated to do. It's your calling."

He could see Larry thinking it over, so he continued. "My touch will stop it, but only for ten minutes. Then you must perform some work. I can help you, but if you don't, you will live this painful life. For what? To go back to a wife who really does not care about you."

Larry was now shaking all over, from both anger and the cold. Through his chattered teeth, he managed to say, "To live, dad. To live my life! To enjoy its bad times and good times. To have a choice to travel or to stay home. Freedom."

How do you explain to Death that life is worth living, no matter what? Deep down, Larry knew he could stick it out. He might not have always been a winner, he might not have been the jock or star kid in a play at school, but he could push through the pain. If he had learned anything from his past, it was that he was great at taking crap from others, at being the underdog, at being the last one picked for the team, and at suffering. And despite all of his setbacks, he would hold his head up high and still show up for school the next day. The kids who always got As on their papers would break like a twig at the first sign of adversity. They had to be given medical attention from the school nurse when they occasionally got a D. But Larry made Ds all the time, and he still went back to school for another round of torment. He could take whatever anyone threw at him; he never dished it out like the other kids, but he could take it. And he could take this. He would overcome. His life had sucked, but it did prepare him for his present ordeal.

Death was hoping that Larry would grow tired of the pain and give in. But he could see that Larry was a fighter. He wasn't the kind of fighter who attacked others, but he was stiff-necked and would persevere. He was going to try to stick it out for seven years. But Death had to try. "Son, why would you want to go back to where you were when I found you? You hated your life, but you didn't want to do anything about it. You weren't taking ownership over yourself. It's only now, after I've found you, that you want your freedom back. You surrounded yourself with people who controlled you. How did you have any freedom with a woman like Pam? Or with your boss? You didn't. You chose to be around them so that when your life sucked, you could blame it on someone else. It wouldn't be your problem. Because someone else made the choice for you. Is that freedom?"

Larry's cold spell was dying down some now, and the pain in his back was completely relieved. He turned sideways in the chair, without looking at his father. "I had more freedom than I do now. Your freedom comes with the pain of taking lives. I've just traded servitude to my wife and boss for servitude to you. I don't call that freedom either."

Death realized he had reached a dead end, but he could be as pig-headed as his son. "I'm not getting anywhere with you. Fine. Stay here. Pass your time in a basement. Read your book. Highlight the sections that you experience. I'm done trying to make you come to your senses."

Larry frowned. "Why, dad? Why this? Why me?"

"I don't know, son. Why is one child born to a crack addicted mother only to die of hunger while another is born to a posh Fifth Avenue socialite? Why you? Why *not* you? Why should this cup be passed on to someone else?" Larry's dad was tired of being the nice dad, it was time to be more upfront with Larry. He understood what Larry was going through. After all, he had been in his shoes years before.

But, it was time for Larry to step up and take responsibility, as he had done. "Don't forget, son: you still have to determine the fate of your own son. You can take up the cup and pass it on to your son one day, or he will lose his life. In choosing what you call your 'freedom,' you condemn your son to die."

Larry glared at his father. This was getting heavy. Even if he made it through the seven years of pain and torment, he would lose his son no matter what. But, at the same time, he didn't want his own son to have to go through this one day as well. In choosing his own freedom, he was limiting his son's future freedom to choose.

Death could see that Larry was deep in thought. "You might find this hard to believe, but I do care about you. And it pains me to see you like this. Because of your calling, you have been spared from many of things. And now they have come back with a vengeance."

Larry listened to what his dad said. Maybe his father didn't want to be doing this either. Maybe he had chosen to follow the calling for *his* sake. Larry sighed. "Why is there so much pain in the world? Why do people have to hurt and get hurt? Why do some pick pain when other get it dished to them?"

Larry's dad knew it was starting to sink in. He was starting to understand. "Why is there so much joy and happiness? What is hot if you don't know cold? Why do people only enjoy happiness, freedom, health, and love after it's gone? Today, you're fighting for a life with a woman who made you miserable two days ago."

Larry understood what his dad was trying to tell him now. Certain things just are the way they are. There's no answer for any of it. Sometimes, you can't change things. You can't bring back a lost love one. You can't choose who your parents are. And, Larry couldn't change his calling, no matter how hard he tried.

"Has anyone ever told you it is rude to answer a question with a question?" Larry joked.

Both men chuckled. Larry's chills where gone, and he was relatively pain free. Unfortunately, as soon as he noticed this fact, his face started to hurt. He felt like someone was jabbing shards of glass into his face. He reached for the book, saying aloud to himself, "painful jabs to the face…painful jabs to the face…page thirty-five." He flipped to the correct spot. "Trigeminal Neuralgia? 'The Suicide Disease' may be the most painful condition known to medical science. Trigeminal Neuralgia, also known as 'tic douloureux,' is a disorder of the trigeminal nerve, which is the fifth and largest cranial nerve. TN produces excruciating, lightning strikes of facial pain, typically near the nose, lips, eyes, or ears. A less common form of the disorder called 'Atypical Trigeminal Neuralgia' may cause less intense, constant, dull burning or aching pain, sometimes with occasional electric shock-like stabs. Onset of symptoms occurs most often after age 50, but cases are known in children and even infants. Something as simple and routine as brushing the teeth, putting on makeup, or even a slight breeze can trigger an attack, resulting in sheer agony for the individual. TN is not fatal, but it is universally considered to be the most painful affliction known to medical practice. Attacks of trigeminal neuralgia are intermittent. They can last from a few seconds to about a minute. The pain varies from an occasional mild twinge to frequent, severe, electric-shock-like pain. Pain is in the facial area, but usually only one side of the face is affected. Remission is less common the longer you have the disorder."

As he finished reading the section, an excruciating shock rocked Larry's face. He screamed out in pain, rolling on the floor as his body jerked with each new jab. He ran to the bathroom and splashed water on his face, as if he could wash away the imaginary glass shards.

"I'm not enjoying this, either, watching you suffer like this," Death informed Larry once the pain seemed to subside a bit.

"Oh, and I am enjoying this, Dad?"

Death knew that, as a father, he should be doing more to take away Larry's pain. And, in reality, he was. If only his son would listen to him, the pain would stop. But obviously Larry didn't see it that way. "I am sorry about this, son. But it's not like I had a choice either. I just want what's best for you. I didn't want to have to pass this on to you. I wanted something better for you, but we don't always get what we want. We're only dealt a few cards in the game of life, and it's up to us to play them as best we can." Death sat down on a box. "When I was young, I didn't have a father either. I told myself that, when I had a kid, I was going to be around for everything—baseball games, science fairs, senior prom, grandkids, the whole nine yards. I'm sure you told yourself the same thing too."

Larry nodded.

"I know you want more for your son, Larry. I wanted more for you. Not that you would be a professional football player, or a Hollywood actor, or the president—I just wanted you to have a normal, happy life. But that's not going to happen, and it's not going to happen for your son either. All three of us are faced with a tough decision. Either we walk away from our families to save them, or we stay behind and watch our sons die."

"I can't do it. I can't do this to my son. I want him to live. I thought if I could make take the pain, then somehow I would…"

"Cheat death? Your son's death?"

Larry started to tear up. "Yes. I can't do it. I'll give in. I will learn the trade from you. I give in, dad. I give in."

With that, Death reached over and took his son's hand. Instantly, all pain disappeared and a wave of warmth filled his body.

He followed his father out of the apartment and down the street. He tried to hide behind Death to avoid another nasty incident with the people nearby. "They can't see you anymore, Larry. You're Death again, remember?"

Larry grimaced. Yes, he was Death. And he was sure that his father wasn't just taking him on a leisurely stroll through the neighborhood. He probably had some business to take care of. Sure enough, Death turned up the driveway into a small ranch house. Larry could hear a child crying, protesting because it was not getting its way. The pair walked into the back of the house. As they entered the kitchen, they saw a woman lying on the floor next to a ladder. Above her was an open kitchen cabinet. She must have climbed up to get something and fallen. The shiny tile floor must have been slick enough for the ladder to lose its grip.

The woman was clearly in pain. She had a bloody gash on her forehead from where she must have hit the oven on the way down. "Take your hand, touch her, and let her pass on," Larry's father instructed him. "Show her to the light."

"But what about the baby," Larry protested. "What will happen to it? What if no one finds it in time? We can't take a mother from a baby."

Larry's father hated this part as well, but he knew what had to be done. "That's not our job, son. I don't know what's going to happen to the child. It's up to the humans to take care of one another while they're living. They are the ones with the skills and resources to help each other. We only have the power to guide them to the next life." He could see that Larry still wasn't budging. "Our job is just to clean up what smells of death; nothing more, and nothing less. We don't get to pick who stays and who goes. We don't get to judge. Take her to the next place now, Larry. It's her time."

Larry hesitated.

"You need to do this, or the pain will start again."

With the thought of pain fresh in his mind, Larry knew what he had to do. He also thought about his own son. Larry bent over the woman and touched her shoulder gently.

Instantly, the woman's spirit was standing next to him, leaning over her body. The brilliant light appeared out of nowhere. "Um, ma'am…" Larry stammered. "Your family and friends are waiting for you in the light. You should probably go over there and see them."

She smiled as she saw the hands reaching out for her. She walked towards the door. Maybe this was going to be easier than Larry had expected.

Or maybe not. At that moment, the crying child toddled into the kitchen. Immediately, the woman forgot all about the doorway and her family. Her attention was taken up with her child. She bent down to cradle the little girl, but her arms went through her. She wasn't able to touch her. The woman began to panic. She frantically reached for the child, waving her arms about. "I can't leave my child," she cried.

Larry wasn't sure how to handle this. "You can't do anything about the child now. You must go to your friends and family."

That didn't seem to work. He didn't think it would.

"I have to watch over my child," she insisted. "I can't go."

The woman was looking around the room wildly at this point. The door, her baby, the hands, Larry, his father…it was all just too much for her to process.

"Who is he?" She shot a sinister look at Larry's dad. "What is he here for? He's not taking my baby away from me!"

Larry sighed. "Listen, I'm new at this. I don't have all the answers to your questions. I'm not here for your child. I'm…"

Thankfully, his father stepped in to relieve him. "Miss, we are only here for you. And help you go to your loved ones who await you."

"What do you mean, only for me? He is learning like a job? You're Death? You just kill people! What else can you learn?"

Death knew that he had to cool her down and get her into the light. Time was ticking away and it needed to happen soon. He gave it one last try. "Ma'am, that's the last of your worries. Now, you have to go into the light or stay here. If you stay here, it will be some time before you can go again. You can't really help your child. Only watch her. For the most part, you will be powerless. And you can watch her just as well from the light."

This just seemed to do more harm than good. "I don't care. I must do what I can. I just want to help my child in any way. Will she be okay?"

The men didn't know what to say.

"We don't really know," Larry told her softly, "but you need to go to the light now if you're going to go. Please trust me on this. Go. Your family and friends want you in the light."

Once again, this didn't seem to do any good. The woman dropped to her knees, so that her face was right next to the child's. "I'm here. I'm not going any place. I'm here for you, my baby."

It was a lost cause. She wasn't going into the light no matter what either of them said. The light began to fade away, as did the hands reaching out for the woman. The room grew colder, and Larry and his father walked out of the house as the baby crawled on top of its dead mother's body.

Larry felt weird about what just happened. As they walked away, he kept turning back to see if someone would enter the house and find the child. But no one had by the time they rounded the corner towards the park.

The two found a bench in the park under a shady maple tree. As they sat down, Larry was still worried about the woman who hadn't crossed over. "What's going to happen to her? Can she ever cross over, or is she stuck here forever?" He asked.

"She can cross over, but only when she's ready. We can show them the light, guide them towards it, but we can't make them go if they won't. Each day that passes for her here on earth will become more and more frustrating. She will feel lost, but it will become even more difficult for her to go. The newness and freshness will give way to discontent and hopelessness. But, as with anything you spend too much time doing, it will be home, her comfort zone. And she will not want to leave, because that's all she understands now, it's all she has."

Larry had never considered any of this before. He thought about the poor woman roaming around for all eternity. "Will she ever leave earth?"

"Yes, someday. But the question is how long? She could walk the earth years after her daughter is gone, forgetting she can go. Maybe she'll start whispering in people's ears, helping them out by acting as a conscience. If she does this, the people she whispers to will know her life as if they lived it, and feel as if it was their life at one time. Some call it reincarnation. But really it's just lost souls, whispering in their ears and trying to live again through the person they whisper to."

Larry's dad enjoyed this part, being able to teach his son. This was the good part of his job. "For many that have much on earth, it's hard to leave it behind. So they try to hold on and control someone else's life. For those who are rich, it's hard to make the jump. Like the Bible says, 'It's easier to get a camel through the eye of a needle than a rich man to get into heaven.' The doorway is the eye of the needle we have to get them through. But sometimes, as you've now seen, they don't want to. They run back to what they had while living. The richest are the hardest to get to go into the light. But the man who carries out the king's crap is more than happy to leave."

Larry and his dad laugh at that thought. "Do they know they're dead, when they're roaming the earth?"

"I'm not wholly sure. But she certainly doesn't want to recognize that she's dead. .How can she understand something so much bigger than life? To her, Death could be a friend that brings peace, a treasure that can't be purchased. Or, he could be someone who removes pain her physicians cannot cure. But now she will have no peace. And each day she will live the pain of not living."

Larry was shocked at how much his dad knew. He understood what most people searched a lifetime to find. Would he ever have that much knowledge? He supposed it would help being Death. But he still didn't know so much about how this all worked.

"The knowledge will come with more experience," his father informed him. "We are there at the time of death. We know how it happens. We see people at their best and worst. But we can't judge them. We just help them jump from one world to another. Be it good or bad." He looked at a flock of geese flying overhead. "We also get to see behind the veil of the great Oz. We see crime. We see war. We see murder. But we also see love. We see hope. We see faith.

"When I first began the calling, I took a man who had been shot during a robbery. Years later, I took that same robber, lonely and living in prison. It takes time to understand the bigger picture. We see families reunited at someone's death. We break up families at someone else's death. We call on people ending their lives early, which only begins their problems. We see it all, son. We learn a lot, much of which I wish I could share with the living."

It was time to move one. There was much work left to be done. Death stood up, enjoyed the sun shining on his face for a second, and made a hand sign for his son to follow along.

"By the way," he said as they walked along, "I loved thick crust pizza."

"What?"

"Thick crust pizza. You wanted to know what I liked to eat when you lit the candle with Pam."

Larry smiled. That seemed like a lifetime ago. "Thick crust pizza, huh? I would have guessed hemlock."

Chapter Seventeen
The House Always Wins

Larry looked over at the old man sitting next to him on the park bench. Twilight was nearly upon them. Larry's narrative had taken longer than either of them had expected.

Larry finished his line of thought. "You know, you helped me learn something today. You talked about gifts. We all have gifts, powers to varying degrees. And everyone has at least one gift, which is your particular piece of power. Acknowledging that I did have power was one of the major factors of why I'm here today, what I am today."

The old man was silent, and the two sat there enjoying the changing hues in the sky as the sun sank over the treetops.

"That's one hell of a story. It all makes so much sense to me now." As much as he hadn't wanted to speak to Larry at the beginning of their day, he was glad he had. It was nice talking to him. He felt at peace, like the great mystery that had plagued him for so many years was solved. In some ways, it was.

"Thanks for listening. I don't get to talk too much now that I have accepted my life's calling. I guess "life: is a funny little word for someone who lives between two worlds. I suppose it's not my life calling me to walk the earth, cleaning up souls. I prefer to think of myself as a poet."

The old man just sat back, still gazing at the fading light. But Larry could see from the old man's eyes that he was scared. If he hadn't already guessed why Larry was there today, he should have figured it out by the end of the tale.

"My dad was right," Larry continued. "Most people do try to cheat death. But in the end, Death always wins the game, no matter how it's played. Death can't be cheated forever."

There was an awkward silence for some time. The old man didn't know if he should try to run or hide.

"I just have one question. How did you get the birthstone keychain? I know you have it."

The old man lowered his head like a child who just got caught with his hand in the cookie jar. "After you wife reported you missing, I went to check out your apartment. I saw it lying next to the candle. I picked it up as evidence. I guess I just kept it all these years. I don't know why exactly. You can have it back if you want it." The old man fumbled in his jacket pocket, forgetting that it had fallen on the ground earlier.

Larry just shrugged. "It's not mine anymore. I can't own things. Part of the job description."

"Well, I guess it's time to go."

"I suppose so."

The old man stood and walked towards the bright light that was blazing in front of the bench.

"Thank you for the talk," Larry called out as the man walked away.

"Thank you for the extra time. I'm sorry I suspected you all of those years."

Larry pointed him towards the light, urging him forward before the doorway closed.

The old man took a step closer before turning back one final time. "What about your son? What happened to him? Did he live?"

In the beginning, Larry had stopped by to watch Pam and his son frequently. But it wore him down, not being able to talk to her or help her. There was so much he wanted to tell her. Once, he found her crying while looking at their wedding picture. That shocked him. He hadn't gone back after that.

He just shrugged. "Not sure."

The old man had gotten plenty of answers today. Larry was sure he had hundreds more, but that was life. The old man smiled and nodded. He turned back to the arms stretching out from the light and walked in.

Larry smiled too as the light faded away. He felt at peace. He had said what he wanted to tell someone for so long. And now someone finally understood him.

Larry stood up from the bench. Night had fallen completely. He put his hands in his pockets and strolled along. Over the years, he had learned to enjoy his job. He liked most of the places he went and people he met—even if he could only be with them for a few minutes. He walked on. He had places to go, work to do. He wasn't sure what would come next, but it could never compare to the afternoon he had spent with the old man today. Maybe he would stop in and see his son. He could smell his next job floating on the air, guiding him along the road.

Epilogue

It was a nice fall day in the park. Pam was sitting on a park bench, reading the Sunday newspaper. She had skipped over the front page and business sections for the human interest pieces. Next to her, her son was playing with a toy dump truck, crunching its wheels through the fallen leaves.

As he rolled the truck back and forth under the bench, the boy noticed something shiny sticking out from beneath a pile of sticks and dirt. He picked it up and watched the sun reflect of the unique black stone encased in silver. He smiled at the new treasure and smelled it.

"Mommy, I love the smell of fall."

"Your dad did too," Pam replied, not looking up from her paper.

The boy went back to pushing the truck across the ground. "Mommy, I love the smell of candles burning in jack-o-lanterns best."

Pam looked up from her paper. An old man walked by and smiled at them. Pam smiled back.

"Mommy, that man smells funny." Pam dropped the paper. "He smells like Uncle Dick did. You know, right before he died."

Pam scooped up her son quickly. What did he just say? She pulled him closer. When he hugged her back, she felt the stone in his hand. "Where did you get that?" she asked.

She had a wretched feeling in the pit of her stomach. It was as if a big clock somewhere had just started ticking, counting down the days for something. She could feel it in her soul.

ABOUT THE AUTHOR

The author's story behind the story. One seasonable cold father's day, a young man watched as his dad lay dying in a hospital bed from cancer. He begun saying his goodbye's to his dad as he already knew his time was short. Earlier that day the smell of death filled the room and seemed to only be smelled by the young man. The smell only went away after his father passed. The young man never forgot and that smell continued to pop up in his life from time to time with the same outcome of his dad. Years early he smelled it on two friends that passed shortly after. Over the years, he grew into a man. While working as a computers systems manager, the young man began to smell the same smell on one of his co-workers. A month later, his co-worker passed away. In his grief over the loss, he attempted to explain this to his wife. Her first question to him was if he ever smelled it on her. She made him swear to tell her if he ever did. After some time, she changed her mind and made him swear not to tell her of her passing. Time continued to pass and the young man was still unsure of how to cope with this uncommon talent and the losses of those he has come to know and are now gone. He decided to use his limitless imagination and developed this story over the next three years.   This is his story.

A SPECIAL THANK YOU TO YOU!

On behalf of everyone at Freedom Of Speech Publishing, thank you for choosing Life's Evil Twin for your reading enjoyment.

As an added bonus and special thank you, for purchasing Life's Evil Twin, you can enjoy discounts and special promotions on other Freedom of Speech Publishing products. Visit www.fospub.com/vip to learn more.

We are committed to providing you with the highest level of customer satisfaction possible. If for any reason you have questions or comments, we are delighted to hear from you. Email us at cs@fospub.com or visit our website at: http://fospub.com/contact-us-2/.

If you enjoyed Life's Evil Twin, visit www.fospub.com for a list of similar books
or upcoming books.

Again, thank you for your patronage. We look forward to providing you more entertainment in the future.

Life's Evil Twin

By Christopher J. Stone

For more books like this one, visit Christopher J. Stone's website at:
http://christopherjstone.com/

Printed in the United States of America
The publisher offers discounts on this book when ordered in bulk quantities. For more information, contact Sales Department, Phone 815-290-9605, Email:
sales@fospub.com

Freedom of Speech Publishing, Leawood KS, 66224
www.fospub.com

ISBN-10: 1938634756
ISBN-13: 978-1-938634-75-8